ORIGINS
Vol I

Edited
by
Jonathan M. Rudder

*

Stories
by
Jonathan M. Rudder
L. Douglas Rudder
C.K. Deatherage
Becca Lynn Rudder

*

RudderHaven
3014 Washington Ave
Granite City, IL 62040
www.rudderhaven.com

Published by:

RudderHaven
3014 Washington Ave
Granite City, IL 62040
USA

First Softcover Printing, April 2017, RudderHaven
(ISBN 978-1-932060-2-25)

RHU Origins Vol I © 2017 Jonathan M. Rudder & Douglas Rudder
Cover art and design: Jonathan M. Rudder
Illustrations: Jonathan M. Rudder & Douglas Rudder

All Rights Reserved

Neither the artist, the author, nor the publisher make any claim to any and all third-party 3D models, textures, or other materials used in the creation of the cover art. All copyrights for third-party materials belong to the individual creators and/or producers of those materials. Used under license. The artist only claims the copyright of the finished derivative art.

Printed in the United States of America

ISBN 978-1-932060-2-25

No part of this publication may be reproduced, stored in or introduced into a retrieval system, or transmitted, in any form, or by any means (electronic, mechanical, photocopying, recording, or otherwise), without the prior written permission of both the copyright owner and the above publisher of this book.

*For the young and young-at-heart
who have donned their capes
and soared through the skies of imagination*

Contents

Foreword...i

In the Beginning by Jonathan M. Rudder........................1

Lionheart: Light and Legacy
by L. Douglas Rudder...5

Cliffhanger: Old Wounds by Jonathan M. Rudder........39

Kid Comet: Birth of a Comet
by L. Douglas Rudder...55

Speedette: At Her Own Speed
by Becca Lynn Rudder..79

Scions of Starmoor: The Gifting of Penelope Pettigrew
by C.K. Deatherage..127

Scions of Starmoor: Looking Back
by C. K. Deatherage...145

Angels of Mercy: Strength in Numbers
by Jonathan M. Rudder...161

Foreword

Comic books have survived the test of time, inspiring readers of all ages throughout the generations with the escapades of costumed heroes in their seemingly eternal struggle against super-powered villains and criminal masterminds. Nearly thirty years ago, my brother Doug and I had created a tabletop role-playing game utilizing trading cards depicting characters from major comic book franchises (for use at home, and not distributed, of course.) As time went on, we started creating our own characters, developing our own universe of heroes and villains. Eventually, those trading cards went in a box, as we began to find our own universe more personal.

Our game universe unfolded and grew throughout the years, joined by characters created by S.L. Rudder, C.K. Deatherage, Becca Lynn Rudder, and others. With the current trends in film and television and renewed interest in the comic book industry, it seemed an appropriate time

Foreword

to begin sharing *our* universe with the public. However, neither Doug nor I are yet artist enough to pencil, ink, and color full comic books or graphic novels, and so we decided to present our stories in the way we know best: the written word (albeit intermixed with some character images of our making.)

Now, it's true that one of the stories contained within this volume, *Birth of a Comet*, has appeared in print before (*The RudderHaven Science Fiction & Fantasy Anthology I*), but it has been revisited and revised for this anthology. The rest of the works are new, though the character backstories that inspired them existed previously in abbreviated form in game documents and mental notes.

RHU Origins Vol I retells the origin stories of several of our key characters, as well as some new recruits, while introducing some of the themes of our universe. I hope you find our offering enjoyable . . . and perhaps leaving you wanting for the next chapters in the RHU Universe.

Jonathan M. Rudder
Managing Editor
RudderHaven

RHU:
In the Beginning. . . .

by

Jonathan M. Rudder

All is dark. Not dark like a starless night, but a pitch blackness, devoid of any light. It is the silent darkness that precedes a storm.

Tap . . . tap . . . tap. . . .

The slow tapping echoes through the void.

Tap . . . tap . . . tap. . . .

Footsteps. Footsteps on concrete.

The sound fades to silence.

Click . . . buzz . . . hum. . . .

Let there be light. A smirk crosses unseen lips.

SCREEEEEE! SCREEEEEE! SCREEEEEE!

Loud, screeching sirens blare. Flashing red and yellow lights spring to life, lining the empty darkness, barely illuminating machinery, girders, and a smooth, empty floor.

At the center of the commotion stands a single individual, silhouetted by the emergency lights. The slight figure wears a trenchcoat and fedora, brim pulled low, hands shoved into the pockets, like the protagonist of an old B detective film.

The figure raises its head. The lights play across the intruder's dark eyes, the soft eyes of a woman or very young man. The eyes scan the wall directly ahead. A metallic box sporting a single, large, unmarked red button sits in a shallow alcove. Shielded cables run from the box back into the wall.

The figure steps forward and gently caresses the button, eyes beaming. *This is it. The answer to all of the world's problems. The 'easy' button.*

The intruder's eyes lower, filled with sorrow and regret. The intruder's hand draws back for only a moment before returning to its original position.

The floor begins to vibrate, a low rumble echoing through the great, empty chamber, muffled by the sirens and the solid walls. The rumble gradually increases in volume, and the room quakes. A large portion of the ceiling at the far end of the chamber collapses in an explosion of dust and rubble.

The figure slowly turns to observe the ruin, hand flattening gently against the button. Light pours through the smoke and dust, silhouetting a host of figures of varying size and gender.

"You took longer than I expected," the intruder calls out in a pleasant, tenor voice. "I didn't even try to circumvent the alarm system."

A tall man with a flowing cape and a sword that shines through the cloud of dust, steps forward from the rubble and debris. His strong voice carries an air of authority as he responds, "Step away from the device."

The intruder pauses to consider the order, hand still poised over the button, then replies in a gentle voice. "No. No, I don't think I will."

The newcomer takes a step forward, and the intruder leans on the button.

The sword-wielding man raises his empty hand to forestall the intruder's action. "Do you even know what this machine does?"

The intruder half-smiles. "Of course. It is the proverbial doomsday device, a safeguard against the extraordinary powers that permeate our universe. It generates a stream of anti-matter and projects it across all known planes. The anti-matter consumes everything, until the universe and everything in it ceases to exist."

The hero gasps. "Why are you doing this?"

"Do you really have to ask?" comes the intruder's gentle reply. "This world—this universe—is hopelessly corrupt. You believe you're heroes, but you're not. You're not even the first to go by that name.

"Throughout history, men and women of great power have risen up to be called heroes or even gods . . . but never have their intentions been guided by the greater good. Always, they have proven corrupt. . . ."

The hero reaches a hand toward the intruder. "No, not all."

The intruder's eyes narrow. "Which ones do you mean? The Extra-planars that fancy themselves gods?

"The masked vigilantes? Almost every one of them, past or present, is a brutal murderer with little regard for life.

"The Patriots? They're little more than puppets for evil and corrupt politicians.

"The Altered? The Genates? . . . Yourself?"

The intruder's head shakes slowly. "Not even you. You're motivated, like the rest of them, by the thrill of action, the allure of power, the praise of the people you claim to protect . . . and you don't even realize it.

"Every one of you, whether you know it or not, are no better than the EPs. You play God with people's lives . . . and no one has the right to play God."

Silence follows the last echo of the intruder's monologue. In that moment, the army of heroes stands paralyzed. The faces—those not covered by masks or helmets—reflect shock, sorrow, guilt, anger, disgust. Even their leader stands with his head bowed in thoughtful contemplation.

The hero raises his head and spreads his hands apart. His gaze is firm, steadfast. "You're right. No one has the right to play God . . . not even you."

The intruder's eyes fly wide, then squeeze shut, allowing a single tear to escape, head bowing. The hand on the button shifts away a little, as the intruder rasps out, "Stop me. . . ."

As the intruder's eyes open once more, they are filled with cold rage. ". . . If you can!"

The chamber lights up with a rainbow of brilliant color and the Earth trembles as the army of heroes explodes into action, and the intruder's black-gloved hand purposefully re-centers on the button. . . .

. . . WAS THE END

RHU Origins Vol I

LIONHEART:
THE LIGHT AND THE LEGACY

BY

L. DOUGLAS RUDDER

I have this sword. It's not a normal sword. You see, it doesn't kill people. It knocks them down, it stuns them, it can leave bruises, and has other effects on the human anatomy—but it doesn't kill. It can cut through chains, concrete, bricks, even solid steel. It can block bullets and other projectiles. It can destroy objects, but not people. And I don't know why.

Not that I'm complaining. I'm *extremely* grateful. I just don't understand it.

Maybe I'd better start at the beginning. Not the sword's beginning, just from when I found it. Or when it found me. The sword existed long before I did. It's really confusing, so bear with me.

It was about four years ago, in the aftermath of a storm system that ripped across the US from the Midwest to the East Coast, leaving a ton of destruction in its wake. Well after midnight, our little town—not too far from Philadelphia—got hammered.

Thunder crashed, lightning slashed the night sky, and the house shook in the wind, rattling pictures and dishes with every violent gust. The windows on the west side of the house bowed inward from the force of the gale. Tornado sirens joined the sounds of snapping branches and debris blowing through the streets. Rain and hail pelted the windows and roof.

When the windows bowed in, I figured it was time to get my family downstairs. I bounded up the steps two at a time and reached the top in time to see my wife, Meara, heading down the hall to our daughter's room. I hurried to catch up. Another blast of wind buffeted the house like a battering ram as we opened the door.

Jade, bless her heart, was sound asleep. That child could sleep through the Tromp of Doom. She had that cherubic look that nine-year-old girls get when they are sleeping—or when trying to wrap their Daddies around their little fingers. She, of course, resisted being awakened. She had no idea what was going on and was more than half asleep when we finally got her to sit up.

Meara pulled her covers back, and I got my arms under her and lifted her out of bed. "Up we go, daughter o' mine."

"Don't wanna get up," she mumbled. "It's nighttime. I'm sleepy."

"There's a big storm, Angel," Meara said, stroking Jade's hair. "We need to go downstairs where it's safer."

"M'kay," Jade answered, resting her head against my shoulder. She was out like a light again by the time we reached the basement.

We headed to the laundry room, since it had no windows, and sat down on the floor to wait out the storm. I leaned back against the wall and shifted Jade into a slightly more comfortable position. Meara reached over and took my hand, smiling down at our little girl sleeping in my arms.

"You're a good Daddy, you know that?"

I squeezed her hand. "That's what I want to be, Meara." My eyes met hers. "And a good husband."

She leaned in closer and kissed my cheek. "You are. I love you, Geoff. Forever and always."

"Me too, Meara." Yeah, we're sappy like that. I wouldn't change it for the world.

A thunderclap hit that shook the whole house, and the power went out. We sat there in the dark, holding hands and listening to the storm.

* * * *

The storm left the town in shambles. Power lines and trees were down, debris littered the streets and yards, branches were strewn about. Many houses had significant damage. Luckily, ours made it through with only minor dings here and there, for which I was very grateful.

That house had been in our family pretty much forever. My great grandfather, Josiah Plantageon, built it. He died serving his country in World War II and left the house to his son, who in turn left it to my father. I grew up in that house.

When my parents moved into the Mansion, along with my grandma and younger brother, Dad passed the house down to me as a wedding present. He knew I was not comfortable in high society, especially as a newly married twenty-year-old. I liked the simple, quiet small town life. Meara and I loved that old house.

It didn't really surprise me when Dad and Mom showed up at our door in the morning to see how we were doing. What did surprise me was that Dad brought along a good chunk of the construction team from Plantageon Enterprises to help with the cleanup. He sent his foreman to contact the town officials to see where they could be put to the best use.

I tried to thank Dad, but he just shook his head and clapped me on the shoulder. "This is our home town too, son. Moving to the city hasn't changed that. Let's get to work."

Mom, Meara, and Jade pitched in to help around our neighborhood. Seeing my little girl throw herself into the cleanup effort warmed my heart. What she lacked in size, she made up for in enthusiasm. She rallied some of her friends into what she called "the Kid Cleanup Brigade" and dove in—with Mom keeping a watchful eye and giving guidance.

Dad and I started out in our neighborhood, and then branched out to some of the trouble spots the construction team and city crews identified. We worked late into the afternoon before we called a halt for the day and headed back to the house.

Meara met us on the front porch. She had apparently just gotten home herself, because she was still in her yard-work clothes and had an adorable dirty smudge on the tip of her nose.

After giving me a quick kiss, she said, "Pastor Hargrove called while you were out. He'd like you to come down to the church. The basement flooded, and they're looking over the damage now."

"Why didn't he call me directly?"

She held up my cell phone. "He did. I just walked in the door when I heard it ringing."

I reached down to the empty cell holster on my belt and grimaced. This was the second time that week

I had left the house with my holster, but no phone. I glanced sideways at Dad. "You could have said something."

He smirked. "You wear that empty clip so often I assumed it was a fashion statement."

"Ha, ha," I responded dryly, accepting my phone from Meara. I gave her hand a squeeze. "I'll give him a call and tell him I'm on my way."

I cocked an eyebrow at Dad. "Want to come along?"

He shook his head. "I'd like to, but I have a meeting coming up and need to get back to the office after I collect your mother."

Meara smiled. "She's upstairs with Jade."

As Dad disappeared into the house, Meara drew near and embraced me, resting her head against my shoulder.

"Be careful," she said softly.

That seemed an odd thing to say. I wrapped my arms around her. "What's up?"

Her shoulders lifted in a shrug. She tilted her head back and looked up at me, eyes thoughtful. "I don't know. Just . . . be careful."

I kissed her on the forehead, then again lightly on the lips. "I will."

And I meant it. I should have known better.

* * * *

"Well, I think we've done all we can for now," Pastor Hargrove said, wiping his hands on a rag. At an active age sixty, Hargrove could still turn a wrench and demo a wall with the best of them. Yet even in grubby clothes and with hands grimed from his labors, he exuded the same warmth and grace that he did from the pulpit on Sunday mornings.

Frank Delaney, chair of the Property and Grounds committee that I was part of, nodded his agreement. "The damage isn't too bad. We'll need to replace some drywall and a few pieces of furniture. At least the water didn't get to the furnace."

We hadn't seen water in the church basement for over a decade. The power of this storm had proved too much for the waterproofing, but it appeared the floor drains and sump pump had done an adequate job of dissipating the water quickly. The floors were damp and a little muddy, but we'd managed to clean up the worst of it.

"Let's call it a night, then," Hargrove said. The five of us, including the other P and G members, Hobart Jackson and Janet Lacy, gathered our stuff and got ready to leave.

I reached for my phone to let Meara know I was on my way home, and frowned. My phone was missing. Again.

"Coming, Geoff?" Frank asked.

"In a minute. I think I left my cell phone in the furnace room." I had been using its flashlight app and apparently set it down while poking around the furnace. "You guys go on. I'll do a quick walk-through and make sure the church is locked up when I leave."

Sure enough, I found my phone sitting on a step stool next to the furnace. I scooped it up and started to call Meara when I heard something unexpected: a faint, steady dripping—into standing water. But there was no more standing water; it had all drained out. I listened intently, trying to determine where the sound was coming from. It sounded distant, toward the east side of the basement. Oddly enough, it seemed to be somewhere beneath the concrete floor, which didn't seem possible since I was in the basement already.

"Oh, great," I muttered. If it was under the basement floor, it might be a ruptured underground pipe. I shoved my cell phone in its holster and left the furnace room. I needed to locate the source of the leak pronto.

My footsteps echoed in the stillness of the basement. The empty church above me creaked and groaned as old buildings do. The church was built in the 1930s, before World War II. While we had updated all the wiring and heating and cooling systems, we tried to maintain the original look and feel, the nostalgic atmosphere of the place. Wandering alone in the echoey basement of an aged, creaky church lent an air of suspense to my search.

The dripping sound led me straight to—the Hall of the Secret Door.

Well, that's we called it when we were kids, anyway.

There was a hall between the storage room and the rec room, about fifteen feet long, with no light except what spilled in from the main room. At the end of the hall was a door with a strangely-shaped lock—that no one could find a key for. It had never been opened as far back as I can remember. As kids, we made up all kinds of stories about the Secret Door and what mysteries might lie beyond.

In any thriller, this was the point where the audience would be whispering, "Don't go down the dark hall and open the spooky door!"

So, of course, I started down the dark hall to see if I could open the spooky door.

Armed with the flashlight app on my phone, I investigated the portal. The door was set to swing outward, but the hinges were recessed in the frame so that I couldn't just pop them loose. I pulled out my Swiss Army knife, selected a thin blade, and tried to jimmy the lock. To my surprise, it only took a minute or so before I heard a click and felt the latch release.

My heart fluttered a little as I slowly eased the door open, flashlight phone aimed inward and pocket knife gripped tightly, trying not to let my childhood imaginings get the better of me.

Nothing jumped out at me. The beam from my phone revealed a four-by-four closet—totally empty at first glance. No boxes, no bogeyman, nothing. The *drip, drip, drip* of water sounded stronger than ever, definitely below me, a little to the left of the closet.

I played my beam around the closet until I found a light switch. I flipped it on. Nothing happened. A quick examination of the ceiling revealed why. It was bare. No light fixture at all.

Now it *had* been a long, exhausting day, but this was getting weird. I just followed a dark hall to a locked door concealing an empty closet with a light switch but no light.

I began a more careful search of the closet. The beam from my light swept across a glint of metal. I swung the light back to focus on a metal rod that stood propped up in one corner. I ran my light down the rod's length. It had an L-shaped, multi-sided bend on the end, almost like a three-foot-long, hefty Allen wrench.

"Okay," I murmured, peering at the rod. "You must serve some purpose. Let's find out what it is."

An investigation of the walls showed that, other than the light switch, they were as bare as the ceiling. I turned my attention downward. White tile covered the floor, with an inset pattern in the middle, about three feet square. The tiles in the four corners of the inset were red, with a single black tile in the center. A thin layer of dust rested over it all, except where my feet had disturbed it. I ran my light along the seams of the inset. And there it was.

Near the corner of the right-hand seam nearest the closet door was a small, inch-wide divot in the tile. I hefted the rod and held it like a golf club and slid the L-shaped end into the divot. It bumped against something metal, but did not go into the edge of the tile. I tried angling it back and forth and was rewarded with a soft *click* as it slid into the socket. The rod was tilted forward at about a forty-five degree angle.

My heart rate ticked up a bit as I gave the rod a tentative tug. It didn't budge. Shifting to a two-handed grip, I pulled harder. With a grind, it moved a fraction, then locked up solid. I grimaced. Maybe a little WD-40 would help. I shook my head.

"Come on, Plantageon," I muttered. "You got this."

At six-foot-two with an athletic build, I wasn't exactly small. No way I was going to let this lever defeat me. I rubbed my hands together and took hold of it again, bracing my feet and giving my shoulders a shake to settle into position. With a grunt, I pulled again, muscles straining as I gave it everything I had.

There was a metallic screech as the socket slowly turned, then suddenly it broke past the sticking point and came to an abrupt stop with the rod sticking straight up.

With a *clank*, the inset in the floor popped up about three inches, spilling dim light out from around the edges of the platform. Grasping the right edge of the raised floor, I carefully lifted. It was hinged on the left side and opened with the agonized squeak of disuse. A shaft descended about twelve feet below me, illuminated by a single incandescent bulb hanging from the stonework wall. A metal ladder was affixed to the side nearest the closet door. At the bottom, I could see standing water, but it was only a few inches deep. Faint light shone from a passage that opened to the left at the base of the shaft.

At least I knew what the light switch in the closet was for now. To light a hidden sub-basement . . . beneath an old church . . . that nobody knew about.

"Ho boy," I whispered when I found my voice.

Now would have been a good time to call Hargrove or Dad or Meara—better part of valor and all that. But no, I'm the cat that curiosity will probably kill someday. I clipped my cell phone to my belt and started down the ladder.

With a soft splash, I stepped down onto the flooded floor. The water came to my ankles. It was cool, but not icy. The musty smell of moisture, age, and mildew filled my nostrils. I suppressed a sneeze and surveyed my surroundings.

The short passage opened into a good-sized room, I'd say about fifteen feet across from me and twenty feet long, extending to the left of the entrance. The stonework of the shaft walls continued into the passage, but the room beyond had ceiling and walls of concrete. A little ways into the room, I spotted a trickle of water running down the outside wall. It gathered on a pipe extruding from the wall, ran along a seam in the pipe for a bit, and then dripped down into the standing water below.

I had found the source of the dripping sound . . . and much more.

The church upstairs had been well-maintained with a nostalgic '30s flair, but this room seemed truly frozen in time. Everything from the sparse furnishings to the old knob-and-tube wiring was authentic and clearly untouched for decades. It was like stepping into a history book. I couldn't wait to turn the pages and learn the secrets of this place.

The room was lighted by a couple more incandescent bulbs in fixtures suspended from the ceiling. The wall to my right had a niche cut into it, about four feet long and eight inches high. It appeared empty. All the furniture in the room resided in the front half, near the passage. An aged wardrobe stood against the wall to my left, next to an upright chair and ottoman, flanked by a small end table holding a reading lamp.

A quick check revealed the wardrobe was locked. I toyed with the idea of breaking the lock, but decided to wait until someone more skilled at lock-picking could tackle it. It would be a shame to damage the antique beyond what the water had done.

Across the way, a small wooden desk butted against the wall, framed by a dusty filing cabinet and a hat rack. A yellowed map hung in a frame over the desk. I sloshed my way across the room to check them out.

The map was of Philadelphia, circa 1939. The desk itself was unremarkable, except insofar as it must have been a hassle getting it down that ladder into the sub-basement. Its surface held a lamp; a notepad with brittle, blank paper; a set of fountain pens; and sundry items. A picture of a young woman was nestled beneath the desk lamp. She looked vaguely familiar, but I couldn't place her.

The file cabinet beside the desk was locked. Once again, I resisted the urge to force the lock. This was part of the church's history and not mine to break to satisfy my own insatiable curiosity.

The far end of the room was mostly open floor-space, not counting the ankle-deep water, of course. A couple of pairs of weathered boxing gloves hung from a rack on one side of the room, along with some other boxing-related equipment. It was definitely dated, but I recognized most of the stuff. I dabbled in boxing as part of my self-defense training. Dad had thought it would be a good idea for my younger brother John and me to learn the art of self-defense. I'd never actually had to use the training thus far, but it was good exercise.

On the other side of the room, about three feet out from the wall, stood a six-foot-high wooden post. It looked like it had taken quite a beating—which it probably had, considering the wall behind it held a rack of four heavy wooden swords. I puzzled over the post for a moment, but then I got it. This was a medieval pell, a post used to practice swordplay. Kind of a Middle Ages training dummy. I had seen pictures of one in my medieval history class in college.

What on earth were wooden swords, boxing gloves, and archaic training dummies doing in a hidden sub-basement behind a secret door beneath an old church?

A *shink* like a keen blade swiped against a whetstone startled me out of my musings.

I spun around and then gave a yelp as my feet slid on the wet concrete and shot out from under me. I landed flat on my back with a *splash* on the flooded floor. Coughing and sputtering, I flailed about trying to get back to my feet, but only succeeded in rising to one knee. I whipped my head around to look back toward the entrance.

There was nobody behind me—which should have been obvious, because any would-be attacker would have been laughing himself silly by this point.

I shook my head, water dripping from my hair . . . and arms, clothes, and pretty much everywhere else. One drop clung to the tip of my nose. I blew it off and grimaced. When I got home, I knew Meara would ask me why I was soaked. I would tell her, and she would laugh. A lot. And then she would laugh again.

I carefully regained my feet and shook my arms to dislodge excess water. Running my hand through my drenched hair, I scanned the room to see if I could spot what caused that weird noise.

A faint glimmer caught my eye, emanating from the niche I had noticed when I first entered the room. My brows furrowed. I was sure that niche had been empty before.

Sloshing across the room again, I peered into the shadowed nook. A sword lay on the concrete shelf, silvery light shimmering along its edges, reflecting off the bronze crossguard and pommel. The grip was wrapped in black leather. It was a simple sword, yet seemed to radiate a beauty and power beyond its plain appearance.

Barely breathing, I reached out and grasped the hilt and began to lift the sword. A jolt of energy surged up my arm and into my shoulder. With a shout, I dropped the sword and jerked my hand away. The sword clattered against the concrete as it landed back on the shelf.

My right arm tingled with the after effect of that jolt, and my heart hammered in my chest. I gaped at my right hand, flexing my fingers to make sure they were all still there. There were no marks on them, no burns or redness. What on earth had just happened?

I stood there panting, willing my heart to slow to a more reasonable rhythm. Rubbing my hand and arm, I dropped my gaze back to the shimmering sword.

Whatever had caused that sensation in my arm, it was not electrical in nature—which was good, since I was still standing ankle-deep in water. It would have fried me on the spot. The pain normally associated with an electric shock had been absent as well. The surge had not been painful. In fact, it had felt almost exhilarating in a strange way.

Slowly I reached for the sword again. I did not touch it this time, but just held my hand near the grip. A warmth and energy seemed to emanate from it with a quiet intensity, like a power that had been contained too long and yearned to be released once more.

I pressed my lips together. *Come on, Plantageon,* I admonished myself. *Don't let your imagination run away with you.* There had to be a more rational explanation.

Perhaps the sword contained some sort of radioactive substance. Now there was a cheery thought, considering if that were the case, I'd just been directly exposed to it. That seemed unlikely on the face of it, but it would be worth checking out.

I'd need the proper equipment to do any real analysis. And the best place to get that equipment was from our labs at Plantageon Enterprises.

I headed back to the shaft and started up the ladder. My feet felt pruny inside my work boots. I could only imagine what they looked like after over an hour in the water. When I reached the trapdoor, I noticed a handle on the underside of the door and a latch that could be opened from the inside. Something to keep in mind for future forays into the underground hideaway.

Because that's what it was: an old hideaway. Looking back, I still feel embarrassed that I didn't figure it all out sooner. My only excuse is that it was late, and I was tired and mystified and not thinking clearly.

Closing the trapdoor, I wondered how to get it to settle back down into the floor of the closet. Finally, I just stepped on it and pressed down. It sank into the floor until the latch clicked. The lever tilted back to its starting position. I popped the rod loose from its socket and set it back in the corner.

I hesitated before closing the closet door. Would I be able to jimmy the lock again? I decided to go ahead and lock it. Until I could find some answers about the energy radiating from the sword, it would be best to keep the sub-basement hidden for everyone's safety.

Before I headed out to the lab, I figured I'd better call Meara and let her know I was going to be late. I grabbed my phone from its clip, only to find it waterlogged by my splashdown in the sub-basement. It wouldn't power on. Great.

I ended up calling her from the church office.

When Meara answered, I said, "Hello, Beautiful."

"You're still at the church," she said flatly.

"No fair. You peeked at the caller ID."

"Hush," she retorted. "I've been calling you for the past half hour. Where have you been? Supper is in the oven."

"Sorry, hon. My phone is dead."

"Didn't you charge it?"

"Yes, but that was before it drowned."

"Oh, this ought to be good."

"Later," I said. "Don't wait supper for me. I need to run out to the office before I come home."

"What's wrong, Geoff?"

I paused. I don't like to keep anything from Meara—ever—but while it was unlikely anybody would be listening in on our call, this was not exactly a secure line. Maybe I was being paranoid, but I had this strong feeling that I should not discuss what I'd found over an open connection.

"I made an odd discovery tonight, Meara," I replied. "I think it's worth looking into. It may take a while to research. Don't worry, I'll either pick up some take-out in town, or I'll heat up leftovers after I get back."

"You're sure you're okay?" Meara asked, her voice tinged with uncertainty.

"I'm fine . . . as far as I know."

"That's reassuring," she said dryly.

"I'll tell you all about it—in detail—when I get home. I just need to check on something first."

There was silence on the other end for a moment. I could tell Meara knew I was holding something back.

"I want to hear the *whole* story when you get back. Don't do anything ridiculous." She gave a little sigh. "I love you, Geoff."

"I love you, too, Meara. Trust me, this story will knock your socks off."

"At least," she said with an ornery lilt in her voice. "Don't be too long."

Sometimes Meara doesn't play fair.

* * * *

The sun sat low on the horizon when I came out of the church. Streetlights were already on. In the glow of the parking lot light, right by the front door, sat a white Mercedes. Its owner—a tall, elderly man dressed in an immaculate, gray suit—leaned against the side of the car.

Nathaniel Blakely, a member of our church, seemed to appraise me with a critical eye as I approached. His white hair and neatly-trimmed beard framed a lined, but still handsome face. He walked with a knobby cane that looked more like a shillelagh than a walking stick.

Blakely had been attending the church since well before I was born. He rarely spoke, but when he did, people listened. He had a quietly commanding presence that brooked no nonsense, but he never raised his voice in ire. He appeared to be in his early seventies, though he said he was older than that—without divulging his true age, of course. Some of our younger members hoped that they would still be in as good shape as old Nathaniel when they reached his age.

"Good evening, Mr. Blakely," I said, holding out my hand. "What brings you out here tonight?"

Blakely ignored my hand, but stood up straight, both hands clasped around the top of his cane, which was planted firmly on the pavement before him. He tipped his head slightly in a polite nod. His eyes were bright and vibrant, almost youthful, yet a lifetime of wisdom swam in their depths.

"Finally," he said softly. "The Light has been re-awakened. Its former bearer would be glad to know it has remained in the family, though I told him it would be so. It is tied to your House, as long as one worthy of the path can be found therein."

"Excuse me?" I said.

Blakely gave me a cryptic smile. "Come now, Geoffrey. I know what you have seen tonight." He lifted his hand and gestured to me. "The Light has come to you now. Use it only for good, to protect the innocent and vanquish evil."

The old man's gaze bored into mine, as though he could see into the very depths of my soul. "Never wield the sword in hatred, lest the Light be extinguished."

This already weird evening had just taken a sharp turn into the utterly bizarre. How did Blakely know about the sword—and how did he know I had seen it? I tried to press him further, but he waved me off.

"It is enough for now. You have had a busy day, and I must be going. We will speak again." He opened the door of his car and started to get in. He paused mid-motion.

"Oh, one more thing," he said, feeling around his pockets. He looked perturbed for a moment, then his eyes lit up. "Ah, there you are!" He reached into his inner suit coat pocket and pulled out a small box.

"You might find this useful," he said, tossing the box to me. With another nod, he got into his car and left.

I stared stupidly at the box in my hand for a moment, my brain doing cartwheels from too many shocks coming so close together, then lifted its lid.

Inside was a strangely-shaped key—a match for the strangely-shaped lock on the Secret Door.

* * * *

The cool night air, combined with the dampness of my clothes and hair, sent a shiver through me as I drove along the highway toward Philadelphia. I turned the heat up a bit and settled back in my seat.

My mind was still whirling from the day's events. The hidden room, the appearance of the sword, Nathaniel Blakely's cryptic pronouncement all had me totally off-balance—and excited and intrigued. I like to understand things, to analyze problems and provide solutions. This was beyond anything I had experienced before.

Where did the sword come from? I mean that in both the sense of its origin and how it had appeared in the sub-basement. While rational thinking told me it had to have been there all the time, my mind's eye kept seeing an empty niche in the wall. Most likely a trick of the shadows, but unsettling nonetheless.

Who had its "former bearer" been? I had an inkling of an idea, but it was too incredible to even consider, especially in light of Blakely's comments. I wish I had taken a closer look at the details of the sword earlier.

And then there was the sword itself. What caused the shimmering effect on the blade and that intense surge of energy that hit me when I picked the sword up? Of all the mysteries, that was the most immediate concern. The thought that I may have been exposed to radiation of some kind worried me, but only a little.

I couldn't explain it, but I doubted I was in any real danger. Still, it would be best to make sure. Hence my trip to Plantageon Enterprises.

Even after more than a decade, the existence of Plantageon Enterprises seemed surreal. Seeing my Dad go from being a small-town wannabe inventor to the head of his own multi-million dollar tech corporation was unbelievable. None of us saw that coming.

Don't get me wrong; Dad has always been brilliant. He attained a Bachelors in Mechanical Engineering, a Masters in Aerospace Engineering, and a Doctorate in Physics. When I was a kid, he was often tinkering around with various gadgets and drafting some amazing designs. He was a dreamer, but for so long the breaks never seemed to go his way.

While studying for his Physics degree, Dad took an Engineering position at a local tech company. The work was routine, but he spent extra hours refining his ideas, hoping to finally make them a reality.

None of his major concepts got past the design phase. They were too visionary, too involved, and the higher-ups couldn't see a fast enough return on investment to justify the expenses to the stockholders. So Dad muddled along, toeing the company line and doing what he could to innovate within the boundaries set out for him. He did have the foresight to convince the company to sign the rights to his "failed" projects back to him, since they considered them of no use anyway. He still had a good relationship with them, but his vision and theirs did not match up.

He continued working on new ideas on his own time, but was unable to secure grants or investors to make them a reality. He was pretty much out of luck.

That is, until the day old Eideard MacDonaugh showed up on our doorstep. We knew about Eideard—pronounced AE-jard—from Grandpa Josiah's letters. The Scotsman had fought alongside my great-grandfather in World War II, as part of an Allied special operations team. Grandpa had described him as a big, blustery bear of a man.

Even in his late seventies, the description still fit. With his booming Scottish brogue, MacDonaugh informed my father that he had been keeping track of our family since the war, in honor of his friendship with Grandpa Josiah. He told Dad that through his contacts in the States that he had learned of Dad's conceptual designs, and they intrigued him.

He then declared that he intended to fund Dad's research and offered to act as a business consultant until

Dad had everything up and running—provided Dad would pick his own engineering team and head up the company himself. In other words, he would provide the financing and advisory business acumen, but it was up to Dad to make his concepts a reality. The success or failure of the company would rest with Dad.

MacDonaugh ended up accepting the position of Business Manager and served the company for seven years before he passed away.

Dad's designs led to the launch of a new space station dedicated to research and development, as well as the first self-sustaining Lunar Habitat. With his vision and the team he assembled, my father produced a variety of unlikely but useful new inventions—including a few I did not find out about until after the sword turned up.

* * * *

Darkness had fallen, but the city still bustled with activity. I stopped at a gas station at the outskirts of the city to fill up before heading across to the lab. Plantageon Enterprises itself was on the outskirts of Philadelphia, having moved to a vast new complex a few years ago from its original offices in the heart of the city, where it had been known as Plantageon Designs, Inc.

As I waited for the pump to shut off, I noticed a young woman walking down the sidewalk on the other side of the street. She looked apprehensive . . . and for good reason. Two rough-looking men strode along a little ways behind her, laughing and calling out rude comments. One carried a wooden baseball bat. She glanced behind her nervously, drawing more derision from her stalkers, then looked across the street. Her eyes widened in fear.

It didn't take long to figure out why. Three more toughs were paralleling her path from this side. As she came up on the entrance to an alley, the three on my side of the street started across . . . one directly toward her, the other two angling ahead of her to cut her off.

The woman shrank back, panic rising on her face, then turned and ran into the alley, looking for an escape.

All five men followed her in.

My cell phone was dead, so I shouted at the gas station attendant to call the police and took off after them.

Be careful, Meara had said. *Don't do anything ridiculous*, she had warned. And here I was, running up a dark alley after a gang of thugs to rescue a young woman I didn't know.

I had no idea what I was going to do when I caught up with them. Even with self-defense training, five-to-one odds—with at least one of them armed with a baseball bat—put me at a serious disadvantage. But I couldn't let them hurt her.

The alley went a short distance, with a dumpster and several trash cans along its sides. Trash and debris littered the ground. It ended in a blank wall; a blind alley. The young woman cringed at the wall, one hand against its surface, one held up to shield her face. As her stalkers drew nearer, she screamed for help. They mocked her screams and advanced on her. I slid to a halt about ten feet behind them.

"Stop!" I bellowed, trying to put as much authority into my voice as I could.

They spun to face me, then looked at each other and laughed again. The one nearest the girl, a snaggle-toothed punk with tattoos covering the left side of his face gave me an ugly grin. "You some kinda moron?"

He motioned to the guy with the bat. "Cave this puke's head in, Ray-Ray."

The one called Ray-Ray stood roughly half a head taller than me and outweighed me by about twenty pounds. He glowered at me and hefted his bat, stepping forward to plant himself within a bat-length from me.

I shifted my weight and spread my hands in a combat stance. Suddenly, my right hand felt warm, and once again energy surged up my arm, flowing into my chest, coursing through my entire body.

The tough with the bat stared at my hand, mouth agape.

"Where did *that* come from?" he squeaked.

My hand gripped the hilt of the sword, its blade shimmering in the shadows of the alley.

"I have no idea," I said . . . then sliced his bat in two.

I pivoted on my right foot and snapped a kick into his midsection, driving him back into two of his companions.

Another thug rushed me. I ducked, dropping my shoulder beneath his charge, then used my shoulder and arm to send him flying over me. He traveled through the air a little farther than I would have expected, crashing down into a couple of trash cans down the alley.

The next in line took a vicious swing at me. I sidestepped it and slugged him in the jaw with the fist gripping the hilt. I heard a crack as he spun around and hit the ground. He gave a little groan and stayed down.

The guy I had kicked was still down, doubled up and moaning. But the remaining two had regained their feet, their expressions angry and wary. With their attention focused on me, the girl slipped around them and made a dash for freedom down the alley.

The leader snarled and snatched up a trash can lid and a piece of pipe from a pile of junk. "You're going down, hero," he growled and launched himself at me.

I deflected a powerful blow from his pipe with the sword, but he smashed into me with his trash can lid shield, knocking me backward. As I fought to regain my balance, he swung at my head. I managed to get my sword up in time, and let his pipe slide down the blade, catching it between the blade and the crossguard. With a twist I ripped the pipe from his hand, then brought my elbow back against the bridge of his nose. He reeled backwards and crumpled in a heap.

I heard the *snick* of a switchblade beside me and twisted to face the new threat. I brought the sword down toward the blade of the last guy's knife. To my horror, my swing missed the target and connected with his wrist instead. I felt a tug as the sword passed entirely through his wrist.

He screamed and dropped to his knees, holding his forearm. I forced myself to look at what I had done, expecting to see a bloody stump. My own eyes widened at what I saw.

His hand was still attached and intact. It hung limply, though his fingers twitched a little.

He goggled at his hand, clearly in shock. "My hand! I can't feel my hand!"

At that moment, I heard a commotion out in the street and saw red-and-blue flashing lights reflected from a coffee shop window. I backed away from the subdued gang and started trotting toward the open end of the alley. There was no way I would be able to explain to the police what had just happened and being caught with the sword would land me in a boatload of trouble.

It was at that moment I realized the sword had vanished, and I no longer felt its energy invigorating my body.

Footsteps rapidly approached the alley from the street. I ducked behind the dumpster near the entrance. A couple of police officers ran past, followed by a small crowd of gawkers. I stepped out behind the crowd and tried to blend in. When a third officer arrived, he shooed us back out into the street. From there, I headed back to my car.

The young woman I rescued stood in front of the coffee shop, being comforted by an older lady, while a fourth officer was conversing over his radio. She saw me cross the street and looked a little confused, but she didn't call attention to me.

The gas pump had shut off by now, and since I had paid in advance, I hung up the nozzle and left. I had paid in cash, thank goodness, so there would be no credit card trail to follow if anyone made the connection between me and the incident. Sometimes being old school comes in handy.

Fifteen minutes later, I strode into the lobby of the Plantageon Enterprises R & D laboratory facility. It was after hours, so few people were left in the building. The night security guard raised an eyebrow at me, but then recognized me despite my disheveled condition and let me pass without comment.

I turned up the corridor toward the main lab. Before I got to the lab, I saw that the door to my Dad's office was open and the light was on. His business office was in the Administration building, but he always considered this one his "real" office.

A sense of relief cut through the fatigue I was feeling at this point. Too many adrenaline rushes and shocks to my system had sapped my strength. I was glad Dad was still here. He and Meara were the two people I could always talk to about *anything*. I valued his fatherly wisdom and guidance . . . and I needed it now more than ever.

Dad looked up from his desk as I entered the office. He leaned back and regarded me with a wry smile.

"Sounds—and looks—like you've had a busy day, Son," he said, nodding at my damp clothes and stringy, tousled hair. "Meara called me and said you were on your way here and why . . . at least as little as you told her."

He cocked an eyebrow at me. "You seem to have taken a detour along the way."

I plopped into the chair across from him. "You don't know the half of it, Dad."

"I may have some idea," he said, indicating the TV on his credenza. The sound was muted, but the image on the screen showed footage of the alley, where I had fought the gang. Police lights were still flashing, and it looked like a CSI team had joined the investigation. It cut to scenes of the thugs being loaded into police cars. The only one who wasn't cuffed was still holding his wrist and looking wild-eyed.

Then it hit me. "Wait, you think I had something to do with that?"

"Tell me about it, Son."

"But—"

He held up a hand. "Tell me about it."

So I did. Everything. From the first drip in the basement, to the secret underground room and finding the sword, to Nathaniel Blakely's strange comments, culminating with the second appearance of the sword in the alley.

When I finished, he said quietly, "Please . . . show it to me."

"I don't know if it works that way, Dad."

"Try."

I held out my hand . . . and there it was. The energy pervaded my body again, but this time it was more like turning on a light switch than a sudden surge. I mentioned that to Dad.

He nodded absently, eyes transfixed on the sword. They held an odd expression of joy mingled with a tinge of melancholy. "The sword is becoming attuned to your physiology. You will always feel the sensation, but it'll become natural to you . . . I think."

"You know something about this, don't you?"

"Look at the pommel, Geoffrey. What do you see?"

The hilt as a whole was mostly unmarked, but on the flat surface of the bronze pommel the image of a stylized lion was embossed. An image I remembered from history books, old newspaper clippings, TV documentaries, and the scrapbooks I used to keep as a child.

"Lionheart," I whispered, awestruck.

Lionheart had been a Hero in World War II. After beginning his crimefighting career as Lionheart, the Champion of Justice, in Philadelphia in the late 1930s, he entered World War II as a founding member of the Amazing Allies, a group of costumed Heroes fighting Axis powers in both the Pacific and European theatres. The tales of the Amazing Allies were the stuff of legend. Lionheart had vanished near the end of the War, never to be heard from again.

I remember playing *Lionheart, the Champion of Justice,* with my neighborhood friends, wielding a toy sword against imaginary foes. Next to my dad, he was my favorite childhood hero.

Now his sword was in my hand.

"How can this be possible?" I asked, gazing in wonder at the emblem. "Lionheart disappeared over seventy years ago."

Dad shook his head. "He didn't disappear. He was killed in action saving his team."

My head snapped around to look at him. "What? How? The Army never said that, they just said he was missing. His body was never found."

"Yes, it was. Only they didn't know it was Lionheart." Dad paused, and looked down as if gathering his thoughts. He pressed his fingertips together, then lifted his eyes back to me. "Only a few people knew who Lionheart was. Not only was he a costumed Hero, he was also a soldier in the United States Army. All of the Amazing Allies were enlisted in the armies of their respective nations. The U.S. Army buried the soldier, without ever knowing he was also the legendary Hero."

"Do you know who he was?" I asked, trembling. I suspected where this was going, but was afraid to believe it.

He nodded. "He was your great-grandfather, Josiah Plantageon."

I let out the breath I had been holding. The picture on the desk in the sub-basement that had looked familiar . . . I realized now that was my great-grandmother, Anna Plantageon. She had been pregnant with my grandpa when my great-grandfather had gone off to war. The hidden room under the church had been Lionheart's base of operations before that . . . and it had been there my whole life, right under my feet.

"How long have you known?"

"Since you were a baby. My father told me when he fell ill, and we were not sure he was going to make it. He wanted to pass on the knowledge to me before he died." Dad smiled again. "Thankfully, he beat the odds and lived to a ripe old age. But his premature revelation will pay dividends now."

Before I could ask what he meant, he went on, "Eideard MacDonaugh knew as well. He even implied that there were old folk-tales hinting that there was a Lionheart—other than King Richard—in the Middle Ages, though that is historically unsubstantiated.

"My father had hoped that he would follow in Grandpa Josiah's footsteps." Dad blushed. "After he seemed unlikely to be the one, I'll admit I hoped that the sword and mantle of Lionheart might pass on to me. When I got old enough to realize I was past my prime, I held out hope for one of my sons. Eventually, it became clear that if it were to happen, it would be you."

That last statement was all too clear.

My younger brother John had become somewhat of a loose cannon, narcissistic, and less than ethical in some of his dealings. Dad and I both had spent time smoothing over the aftermath of John's shenanigans with business partners. I still had hopes for him though. I believed he was basically a good kid that had listened to some bad advice.

"Thanks, Dad," I replied, inhaling deeply. "My mind is reeling right now. I'm still not sure any of this is real."

"You're holding the proof in your hands, Son," Dad reminded me.

It was true. I was holding it in my hands and feeling its effects on my body. I felt more aware, more vital, more energetic—pardon the pun. As I looked into my dad's eyes, I understood both the joy and melancholy I noticed earlier. He was proud that his son had inherited the sword—but he had dreamed of becoming Lionheart in his younger days as well.

Dad glanced down at the sword. "May I?" he asked tentatively.

I lifted the sword up horizontally, letting it rest across my palms. "Go ahead. You've waited a long time to see this day."

Dad started to reach for the sword, but his hand stopped just above the hilt.

"I'd better not," he said wistfully. "It might disappear again."

"Why?"

"Because it is meant for your hand alone. *You* are Lionheart."

I lowered the sword . . . and it was gone again. "I'm sorry, Dad."

He looked surprised. "Don't be, Son. I found my path in life, and I'm happy. This just adds to my happiness. I'm glad for you, Geoff."

Now it was my turn to blush. "Thanks, Dad. I'll try to make you proud."

"I've always been proud of you, Son," Dad said. "Do what's right and just and honorable. That's your heritage."

"I've had a good role model to follow." For the life of me, I could not imagine why my dad had not inherited the sword. He was a noble spirit; no one could be more worthy.

"Besides," Dad said with a mischievous smile. "It's not like I won't be part of the equation. Remember, I've been hoping for this for quite a while now. I may be a dreamer, but I'm also a planner."

A cautious excitement rose in my chest. "What have you done?"

"Mm, I may have constructed a . . . place of sorts. A 'what if' room, you might say."

"You mean like a hidden sanctum?"

Dad grinned. "I call it the Lion's Den. I'm glad it will serve its purpose now. It's loaded with gadgets. You'll love it."

Of course, I wanted to see it right then, but Dad settled me down, reminding me that I had other responsibilities to take care of first.

"Come to Plantageon Mansion tomorrow morning," he said. "Early. Right now, you have a wife and daughter waiting for you at home. The Den's not going anywhere, and it's going to take some time to show you everything. There's also a prototype costume down there. I'd like your feedback on the design . . . since it's going to be yours now."

LIONHEART

Cliffhanger: Old Wounds

by

Jonathan M. Rudder

The bright lights of Boston did nothing to light the rooftops of the brownstones on the Bay. Their dark silhouettes, speckled with lamp-lit windows, made an uneven wall above which could be seen the city lights. At the top of one of the tallest brownstones, a ten-story building, a dark figure crouched, his gloved hands grasping the parapet. Cliffhanger was one of the newest of a host of costumed vigilantes and crimefighters that had appeared in recent years.

His costume was dark—green torso and mask, brown arms and legs, black gloves and boots—designed for use in jungles and mountains, not cityscapes. His full mask covered all but his eyes, which were closed. A black, leather harness wrapped around his torso, holding a series of seven-inch, rectangular metal rods.

He had never intended to become a vigilante—nor did he intend to remain one once his mission was completed—but the circumstances that had created him required that justice be served. His target had been pursued across continents by law enforcement and military of every variety, to no avail. They simply did not know where to look.

But he did. It took him nine years of preparation and investigation, but he had finally located his target—or at least his target's associates—and set his trap. The lure: an ancient Aztec mask that was supposed to hold the key to a vast lost treasure . . . just the sort of item the mercenary coveted. Going through one of the target's associates, Cliffhanger had set up a meet, pretending to be a seller, showing off an Aztec mask he had found during an archaeological dig two years earlier. The meet was to take place on the rooftop below him in less than an hour.

His grip on the edge of the parapet tightened in an effort to stave off the trembling of anxious anticipation that had come over him. Soon, his loved ones would have justice. Soon, the monster that had murdered them and left him for dead would face his judgment. Nine years. . . .

* * * *

An abandoned village along the Amazon River. . . .
Billionaire industrialist and world-renowned electronics magnate Vincent Forest Lake was also known as a great philanthropist and sponsored many humanitarian and scientific endeavors. Among them were the expeditions of French archaeologists Antoine and Renée Delacroix. That started mainly as a favor to

his son, Steven, who was interning with them during his undergraduate studies, but the Delacroixs and Lakes soon became good friends.

That is what brought Vincent Forest to the Amazon. The Delacroixs had discovered an idol in the center of a long abandoned village. It was unlike anything they had ever seen, and certainly not a product of any of the indigenous tribes.

Antoine and Renée were standing with Steven Lake and the Delacroixs' six-year-old son Francois at the edge of a large, cordoned-off hole in the ground at the center of the village, when Vincent Forest arrived. There were a scant few other interns and non-native workers present in the ruins of the old village.

"Sorry it took so long for us to get here," Vincent Forest called out as he approached the archaeologists, bodyguards in tow. "Our native guides abandoned us a few miles back."

"Not surprising," Antoine replied with a light chuckle. "The natives believe the village is haunted. They call it Pûera Taba . . . Bad Place."

"Hi, Dad," Steven said, giving his father a quick hug. He was tall and lean, but a year of fieldwork with the Delacroixs had put some muscle on him. At the age of nineteen, he was not only finishing up his internship, but also his Senior year in college. To call him a prodigy was an understatement. Steven could have become a doctor, a lawyer, a businessman, engineer, or all of the above, and made a fortune larger than his father's in no time, but he had a passion for archaeology, and that is what he chose to pursue.

The elder Lake smiled at his son. "Hello, Steven. So where's the statue you were so on fire about?"

Steven grimaced and waved a hand toward the gaping hole. "There was a small quake last night, and this sinkhole opened up. The idol shattered when it hit bottom."

"We've never seen a material like it," Renée added. Her accent was significantly thicker than her husband's. "Black, with the texture and luster of metal, but extremely brittle."

"That's not the half of it, Dad," Steven said, taking his father by the elbow. "Take a look down here."

Vincent Forest stepped to the cordon and looked down into the sinkhole. A faint gold light shone among the fragmented and splintered remains of the idol, like some sort of phosphorescent paint splattered across the stone below. He glanced over at his son. "Radioactive?"

"Slightly," Antoine replied. "We have a Geiger counter for the rare situations when we do run across potentially radioactive substances during our digs. The radiation doesn't register until the counter is within a few feet of the dust."

Vincent Forest rubbed his jaw. "Wish I'd known. I'd have brought the LRD."

LRD was the acronym for the Lake Radiation Detector . . . an incredibly simplistic name for a highly complex piece of equipment. The rising number of superpowered beings populating the world generated the need for a way to identify and track a vast array of radiation signatures, not simply the presence of radiation and the level thereof. Lake Technologies' LRD was the most sophisticated, containing a complete database of every known form of radiation, including those introduced to Earth by extraterrestrials.

"I'll call for the LRD to be brought in as quickly as possible," Vincent Forest said with a nod. "In the meantime, I suggest we all stay clear of this hole."

The Delacroixs' young son tugged on Vincent Forest's shirt. "Monsieur Lake! Monsieur Lake! Avez-vous apporté moi un cadeau?"

Vincent Forest barked a short laugh. "Bien sûr, Francois. J'ai appréhendé un cataire des biscuits pour vous."

The little boy blinked dumbly at Vincent Forest, then burst into riotous laughter. "Tu es drôle, Monsieur Lake!"

His parents smiled.

Steven raised a brow at his father. "Did you just tell Frenchy you apprehended him a catnip of cookies?"

Vincent Forest winked at his son, then placed an arm around Steven's shoulders. "Come on. Help me get settled, then you can tell me how the dig's been going."

His bodyguards fell in behind them.

* * * *

Night in the jungle brought its own orchestra of animal noises that differed somewhat from the sounds of the day, but even Vincent Forest had visited enough digs that he was accustomed to them. Only a couple of armed guards remained awake, patrolling the perimeter to keep out unwanted predators.

Something small zipped through the air from the surrounding jungle and struck one of the guards. The man fell backwards to the ground, a small throwing knife protruding from his eye.

A woman's scream split the air. Renée Delacroix had emerged from her family's tent in time to see the guard fall. A tall man, wearing jungle fatigues and a brown, leather jacket, stood at the edge of the village. On each breast of the jacket were two sheaths for small throwing knives, one of which was empty. Lower on the right side of the jacket was a larger knife with a hilt shaped like a venomous snake. His blonde hair and scruffy beard were matted with sweat and dirt.

Lightning fast, he pulled two more of the small knives from his jacket and sent them flying at Renée and the second guard. Both went down, clutching their faces, then lay still. Shouts and yells erupted as the tents emptied of their occupants, reacting to Renée's scream. Walking purposefully toward the center of the village, the man whipped his last small knife at a worker, then pulled a Colt M1911A1 pistol from inside his jacket and started firing, quickly, precisely, one bullet to each member of the expedition.

Antoine Delacroix threw himself down on top of Francois. Neither arose.

Steven Lake leapt at the man, grabbing his gun hand and twisting it up. The man jabbed Steven beneath the ribs with his other fist, and as Steven doubled over, kicked him away. Steven rolled towards the lip of the sinkhole.

The man aimed his pistol at Steven and smirked. As he pulled the trigger, Vincent Forest blindsided him, causing his shot to go wide. The man and the elder Lake rolled in a tangle of arms and legs, with Vincent Forest clawing for the gun. The man finally managed to throw off Vincent Forest, who went rolling towards the sinkhole.

As the Lakes clambered to their feet, the man shot them both, sending them tumbling into the sinkhole.

He looked down into the pit. "Heh. Bloody waste for a bodgy idol."

* * * *

Steven awakened to a sharp pain in his shoulder. He drew in a sudden breath and choked as his mouth and nostrils filled with dust. He was lying face down in a pile of dirt and rock. Coughing, he rolled over on his back and blinked his eyes open, which he quickly shut again with a cry. His vision had been met with a brilliant light, like looking at the sun.

He tried to open them more slowly, squinting against the light, but the brilliance was too great. Blindly he patted the ground around him, until his hand lit upon an arm. He drew his hand back.

"Hello?" he said weakly. "Who's there? What happened?"

His voice was answered by a slight echo of itself. Recollection of the attack flooded back to him.

He reached out and grabbed the arm again. "Dad? Is that you? Dad?"

Vincent Forest did not reply.

Steven remembered the gunshots and falling into the sinkhole. He remembered his father falling alongside him. He remembered Renée Delacroix's scream. He remembered the guards and workers falling dead to the ground. He remembered Antoine Delacroix lying in a heap before his tent.

Most of all, he remembered the voice of the gunman, with its distinctly Australian accent. He remembered the gunman's flippant comment at the end before he passed out.

"Dad," he whispered with a sob. He leaned his head down on his father's chest and wept bitterly.

After a while, he calmed down. He sat up and wiped his eyes with his tattered sleeve. Steven tried to open his eyes again. This time, he was able to squint against the light. It was still bright to his vision, but he could see. It emanated from the ground around him.

The dust from the idol, he thought. *Must've gotten it in my eyes.*

"Great," he rasped aloud. "Bleed out, or die from radiation poisoning."

He drew in a breath and looked down at the bullet hole in his shirt. His brow wrinkled in confusion as he pulled back the cloth and viewed the skin below. The bleeding from the entry wound had stopped and had fully scabbed over. The dried blood sparkled with gold flecks.

Steven scooped up a handful of the golden dust and squinted at it. From the pain in his shoulder when he moved, he could tell the bullet was still lodged inside. For a second or two, his scientific curiosity distracted him from the reality of the massacre he had survived. *What secrets do you hold?*

Shaking his head, he dropped the dust and looked up. He could see the jungle canopy above the opening of the sinkhole.

Must be morning. Better get out of here and see if anyone else survived.

He saw a rope dangling halfway down the side of the sinkhole. *One of the cordon ropes. Must've snapped when we fell.*

Steven tried climbing up to the rope, but the loose dirt and rock kept giving way, sending him tumbling back to the bottom. It took time, but at last he reached the rope and used it to climb the rest of the way. As he climbed, he saw a break in the canopy, through which he saw a black sky, speckled with stars, yet everything around him was lit as though by daylight.

I guess the dust did more than heal my wound.

As he stood at the edge of the sinkhole and surveyed the encampment, he was sure he was the only survivor. Nevertheless, he went from body to body, searching for any other wounded.

At last, Steven came to Antoine Delacroix. His mentor's eyes stared blankly from his bloodless face. Steven wanted to cry again. He knew he should, but his tears were spent. He could only feel anger.

Then he saw the small arm sticking out from beneath Antoine. His heart skipped a beat. He rolled Antoine's body back and saw little Francois lying on the ground. The bullet had passed through Antoine's body and into Francois.

Steven scooped his godson up in his arms and screamed at the sky in livid rage.

* * * *

Steven had eventually escaped the jungle, but not before he had buried the dead and made certain no one would ever find the abandoned village or the idol's golden dust. When he emerged from the jungle, he pretended to be delusional and ranted about ghosts and monsters. When he "recovered," he could not "remember" the location of the dig, nor the whereabouts of his father and the Delacroixs.

He spent the next nine years, preparing to hunt down the man who had murdered them. After completing his undergraduate studies, he went on to receive his Master's in archaeology, but also Doctoral degrees in archaeology, physics, and both electrical and mechanical engineering. He devoted his vast inheritance to creating the costume he now wore and became Cliffhanger, an identity he used to track the man who massacred the Delacroix expedition.

At last, he had discovered the identity of the man: Charles Eddy, a mercenary and treasure hunter specializing in the acquisition of rare artifacts . . . often from the dead hands of his victims. Eddy quickly became known among both international law enforcement and underworld organizations as Taipan, named after the venomous Australian snake for his quick and deadly use of throwing knives. Taipan had a perfect kill record . . . until Steven escaped.

Steven used his archaeological expeditions to try and draw Eddy into a trap—and nearly succeeded twice—but always the elusive treasure hunter slipped through his grasp. In the meantime, his costumed persona garnered a reputation as a jungle spirit, as he found himself meting justice out to tribal tyrants and gangs of thugs as he defended the innocent in the deeps of the jungle.

"The snake has come out of his hole," the accented voice of a young teen boy said through the Bluetooth headset built into Cliffhanger's mask.

Cliffhanger raised his head and opened his eyes, which blazed with a golden light. The door to the roof access on the brownstone below him creaked open, and a familiar figure stepped out, strolling cautiously to the center of the roof. Cliffhanger's eyes narrowed. "I have him, Frenchy. It's time to pull this snake's fangs."

"Moreau!" the treasure hunter called out. "You're the one what arranged this meet-up. You have the mask?"

Cliffhanger withdrew one of the metal rods from his harness and held it off to the side. Both ends of the rod split, and small metal plates and filaments extended from the openings, twisting and sliding into place. In a few seconds, the small rod had doubled in length, ending in a spike. He whipped his wrist forward.

The spike launched from the end, with a thin cable attached, spiraling to the wall of the building across from the one where Steven crouched. As soon as the spike buried itself in the brownstone, Steven leapt from the roof. The cable retracted as he fell, allowing him to swing safely to the rooftop below. The cord slid fully back into the rod, bringing the spike with it.

He landed behind his target and whipped out a second rod. This one unfolded like the first, and the two fused together, extending to the length of a staff.

Taipan did not flinch. With his back to Steven, he said, "Dr. Moreau, I presume? Don't happen to have any islands for sale do you?"

"I'll give you one chance to disarm and surrender, Eddy," Cliffhanger replied.

"And why would I do that?" Taipan replied. "If you know who I am, you know I have a perfect kill record."

Steven poised to strike. "*Had* a perfect kill record . . . until nine years ago. Until I walked out of the Amazon."

Taipan slowly turned to face Steven. His face revealed a brief flicker of annoyance, which melted into a half-grin. "Dr. Steven Lake. I'm guessing you're the jungle demon what's been getting in my way the last few years. Though I'm a bit surprised . . . most vigilantes like to keep their identities secret."

"I'm not planning on maintaining this career for much longer," Cliffhanger replied.

Taipan waggled a couple fingers toward Steven's eyes. "So what's up with the spooky eyes? Glow-in-the-dark contacts?"

"Face full of radioactive dust, thanks to you," Cliffhanger commented. "I take it you're not going to surrender...."

Taipan shrugged. "Why should I? I have you outmatched. Compared to me, you're an amateur."

With both hands and nearly imperceptible movements, Taipan let fly the four small throwing knives from the front of his jacket.

Cliffhanger spun his staff, knocking away each of the projectiles, finishing his defense in the same stance from which he started, eyes fixed on Taipan.

Taipan raised a brow. "This could be interesting."

The mercenary went for the pistol in his jacket, and Cliffhanger lunged forward. His staff retracted down to the two small rods, connected by the grappling cord, forming a pair of nunchaku. As Taipan drew his pistol from his jacket, Cliffhanger wrapped his nunchaku around the mercenary's wrist and spun off to the side, jerking the gun from his hand.

As Cliffhanger came out of his spin behind Taipan, he whipped his nunchaku around, whacking the treasure hunter across the side of the head. Taipan collapsed to the roof with a grunt.

Cliffhanger disengaged the rods in his hands and returned them to the harness on his chest. He reached for another of the rods as he stood over Taipan, which formed into a single-bitted axe.

Taipan groaned and rolled his blood-matted head to look back at the vigilante. "Never heard of you killing anyone, mate . . . I don't think you got it in you."

Cliffhanger glared down at the mercenary, his voice lowering to a growl. "For you, I'll make an exception."

As the vigilante pulled his axe back, Taipan rolled onto his back, whipping out the larger knife from its sheathe. The throwing knife buried itself in Cliffhanger's shoulder, causing him to stagger backwards a few steps. Taipan leapt up, kicking the knife deeper into Cliffhanger's shoulder.

The vigilante fell onto his back with a cry, clutching his shoulder. His axe tumbled out of his hand, clattering across the roof. As soon as it came to rest, it folded in on itself, leaving a plain rod behind.

Taipan reached down and wrenched his knife from Cliffhanger's shoulder, eliciting another cry. He sneered at the vigilante. "As I said, bloody amateur. Well, at least I'll get my perfect kill record back."

"No you won't," Cliffhanger gasped back.

Taipan snorted derisively. "You still think you have a chance to beat me?"

Cliffhanger shook his head. "No, but I don't need to. The other survivor will take care of you."

Taipan's eyes widened. "The other. . . ?"

A flash of bright blue light momentarily blinded Cliffhanger. He heard Taipan fall to the roof with a grunt and a thud. He rolled to his feet and kicked the mercenary's knife away.

Smoke trailed up from a black hole in the back of Taipan's jacket. Cliffhanger used his foot to turn the mercenary on his back.

A young teenage boy wearing a full bodysuit and mask in the colors of the French flag stepped to his side.

He aimed a small pistol that looked like something from a sci-fi movie at Taipan's face.

"You were right about one thing, Eddy," Cliffhanger said to Taipan. "No matter how much I want to, I couldn't kill you. I'll settle with seeing you behind bars for the rest of your life."

Taipan grinned. "Nah, not gonna happen, mate. I'll tell the boys in blue who you are . . . they don't take kindly to vigilantes, no matter how benign."

"I don't much care, Eddy," Steven replied. "Maybe we'll be cell mates. At least, you won't be killing anyone else."

Taipan scowled. "Not likely."

With lightning reflexes, Taipan flung his hands up at his two captors, who dodged out of the way. When they realized it was a feint, they returned their attention to their prisoner, only to find that he was gone.

"What now, Monsieur Steven?" the boy asked. "He'll have the police on you for sure."

Steven walked to the edge of the roof and looked out at the inner city lights. "No, I don't think so, Frenchy. We've wrecked his perfect record . . . he wants us dead, not serving a jail sentence."

He looked at his sidekick. "I guess we're not hanging up our hoods just yet."

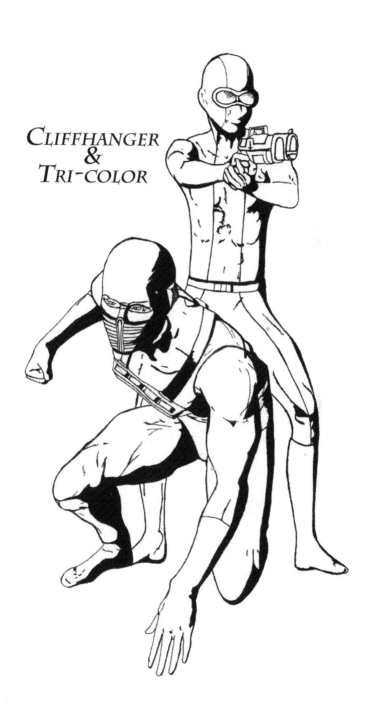

KID COMET: BIRTH OF A COMET

BY

L. Douglas Rudder

"Stay back, or I'll do the same thing to you!"

The youth stood poised, legs apart and arms extended toward his would-be opponents. He looked frightened and confused, but his blue eyes blazed with wild determination beneath his sandy hair.

"Now, Daniel, calm down."

One of the scientists, Dr. Howard Edwards, edged toward him warily, speaking in soft, though strained, tones. Sweat sparkled on his forehead and in the fringe of gray hair that encircled his head.

"We just want to help," he said, glancing past the perturbed fourteen year old at the destruction behind him. Loose plaster and bricks hung from the edges of the ragged hole in the outer wall of the laboratory—a hole that Daniel had made. Dust still hung in the air like a whitish haze, and debris from the blast lay scattered on the tile floor and the lawn outside.

"No!" Daniel stepped back uncertainly, his face taut with anxiety. *Oh, Grandpa,* he thought, *what do I do? I don't want to hurt anyone, I just want them to leave me alone, to let me go . . . home.*

His eyes swept across the scientists and security guards in the spacious lab. He had to escape. The thought of obliterating them just as he had the wall never seriously entered his mind; he could not conceive of intentionally killing anyone. But it seemed like a really good bluff at the time.

"Daniel," Edwards began again. "Listen to reason—"

"Reason!" Daniel spat back. "I'm a prisoner here! I'm not a specimen for your test tubes, I'm a human being."

He took another step toward the gaping hole.

Edwards eyed the opening, slowly drawing nearer. "Daniel, we just want to find out what is happening to you. We mean no harm."

Daniel paused, his determination wavering. The scientist's voice was calm, soothing. Yet when Daniel looked into his eyes it was like watching a viper ready to strike. An involuntary shudder jerked at his shoulders and neck. He turned and fled through the broken wall.

"Stop him!" Edwards shouted. "We have to keep— we have to protect the boy from himself."

His face reddened as he glared after the retreating youth.

* * * *

The grass, still moist with early morning dew, clung to Daniel's shoes as he ran. He could hear the sounds of pursuit behind him.

They'll never take me back. Never! His jaws tightened into hard lines of determination. Then he heard voices and the pounding of feet on the wet grass ahead. More guards . . . they were cutting off his escape route.

He cast his eyes skyward in hopelessness. A hawk soared overhead, with powerful wings beating against the air currents. Daniel yearned for that freedom.

Instantly a bluish light enveloped him. His whole body tingled, as though a rush of energy were passing through him. The hawk seemed to streak towards him—backwards! And then it was gone. Suddenly, he realized that he could no longer feel his shoes nor the damp earth beneath his feet.

Looking down, Daniel was shocked to find that his legs were hardly discernable from the knees down, encased in a blazing blue light that burst from them like the exhaust of a rocket. Yet it was not fire; it was more like a semi-tangible rush of light. Already, Dr. Edwards, the other scientists, and the guards were hardly more than specks on the landscape, receding into the horizon.

"What in the—I'm *flying!*" He almost fainted. The light around him dimmed and he began to fall. "Whoa!"

He roused himself quickly and was jerked upward with a new burst of speed.

To those below, Daniel looked like a comet, his form a mere shadow within an oval of blue light, the energy streaming from his legs forming the tail of the comet. To Daniel, the light around him was like viewing the world through a transparent blue bubble, coloring everything he saw, but not distorting anything. The bubble seemed to emanate from him, accompanied by an intense—

though not uncomfortable—tingling sensation throughout his body.

Through much trial and error, Daniel found that by relaxing he could slow his air-speed. His mind seemed to regulate this mysterious new energy, interacting with it just as it did with the rest of his body. After the initial shock had passed, Daniel realized that this energy did not feel alien, but seemed to be a natural part of his physical being.

Am I some kind of freak? Why can I do this? I know it's a part of me, but how? Where did it come from?

He decided that the first thing he had to do was to get back on the ground before he reached the city. The Fulkmaer/GenTech research base he had just left was located north of Albany, near the Catskill Mountains. As far as he could tell, he had been traveling in a southerly direction, and at the speeds he seemed to be capable of, it would not be long before he would be approaching the outskirts of New York City. At this point, the area he was over still seemed to consist primarily of farmland and small towns; this was where he wanted to come down.

He veered downward like a divebomber. The ground rushed up at him too fast. Pulling his head and shoulders back sharply—and almost hyper-extending his spine—he shot back up into the air, scattering a herd of cows with the turbulence of his passage.

"Agh! How do you land this thing?" he gasped. "What am I saying? I *am* this thing!"

He concentrated on slowing his air-speed and made a second attempt to land. The intended landing site was the pasture he had almost torpedoed before. The frightened cattle had not returned to the west end of the field, so Daniel aimed for that area.

It was not until his closest approach that he knew he had misjudged his speed again, but this time it was too late to change direction. He was going to land . . . one way or another.

It was *another*. He tried to put his feet down, but the energy thrust from his legs skewed his flight path. Cartwheeling horizontally, he plowed into the ground. Bouncing several times across ground that was not nearly as smooth as it appeared from the air, the battered youth finally came to rest face down in a clump of field-grass. The mucky feeling beneath his chest attested to the fact that a cow had been there recently.

For a few moments he just lay there, counting his bones to see if they were all still intact. Nothing seemed to be broken, although his left wrist and elbow throbbed painfully.

All was quiet. The only sounds were the wind rustling in the grass and cattle bellowing in the distance.

He sat up, groaning with the effort. In addition to the pain in his arm, his body was a veritable patchwork of bumps, bruises, scrapes, and cuts. He stripped off what was left of his shirt as best he could, using the rags to clean the rest of the muck off his chest. His nose wrinkled at the smell.

"I've gotten myself into a great mess now," he muttered under his breath. "I'm filthy, banged up, probably have half of New York State looking for me, and no place to go. Daniel Jay Bagby, you've really landed yourself in the fertilizer this time."

He glanced at the tatters of his soiled shirt. "Or something like that, anyway."

Daniel stood up and surveyed his surroundings. The pasture was flat and open, studded with rocks here and there. It was surrounded by an electrified fence, which consisted of three evenly spaced strands of electric wire with one strand of barbed wire above them. North of the pasture was woodland; Daniel could not tell how deep it was.

Next to the west end where he stood was a single-lane, unpaved road that went past the white farmhouse at the south end of the pasture. An old wood barn leaned outside the gate to the east. The cattle stayed near the gate; apparently they would rather be in the barn than in the field with a U.F.O.

He scratched his bare ribs as he pondered his next course of action. Should he go to the farmhouse and ask for help? Perhaps . . . if he wanted to get a door slammed in his face. No shirt, covered with grime, beat up—he looked like a vagrant run over by a combine. He noticed for the first time that his shoes and socks were gone without a trace, and the legs of his jeans were missing below the knees, the remainder being torn and dirty.

He could follow the road in hope of finding a town where he could get help. He shook his head. *Dr. Edwards has probably already contacted the police. I can't go there. Where then? What would Grandpa do?*

The answer came almost immediately in the image of one of his grandfather's old war stories.

The story had to do with an incident during the Korean War when Grandpa Jack had been separated from his unit in enemy held territory. He had heard an enemy patrol approaching and had nowhere to run. "So, Jay," he would say—he always called his grandson by his middle name—"I clumb the nearest tree and whittled a stick until they left."

Daniel smiled wryly. *Okay, Grandpa Jack. A tree it is.*

He headed north toward the woods. He crawled under the fence, wincing and favoring his left arm. Under normal circumstances, he would have simply jumped it, but he was not feeling too spry at the moment.

Plunging into the undergrowth, he made his way to a large tree about twenty yards into the forest. From there, he could still see the road and the farmhouse, but would be relatively safe from view himself.

He leaned against the tree, trying to spot handholds low enough for him to reach. He started to lift his left arm, but a stab of pain brought it back down. He grimaced. His wrist and elbow were noticeably swollen now; he began to wonder if they might not be broken after all. No, he could still move them okay, even though it hurt to do so.

He sprawled on the ground beneath the tree and exhaled deeply. Willing himself to relax, he let the cool wind sooth his battered body. The musty scent of the vegetation around him filled his nostrils. All was peaceful. The music of the birds in the treetops combined with the gentle breeze made him drowsy. His mind wandered as he tried to understand what was happening to him.

There was no one to turn to. When Grandpa Jack died three years ago, Daniel became a ward of the State at the age of eleven, having no other living relatives. He had never known his parents. They had both been employees at the Fulkmaer Corporation before it was bought out by

GenTech. They were engineers and had been working on the development of a new solar energy collector system. Shortly after the buyout, there had been an accident, and Paul Bagby and his wife, Elizabeth, who was three weeks pregnant, had been exposed to high doses of solar radiation. Elizabeth eventually died in childbirth, her husband two months later.

Daniel was raised by his grandpa, Jack Bagby, a widower. Grandpa Jack had been an easy-going man who could be firm when he had to. He had a small farm outside Albany, but it had been sold after his death. Daniel and he had been very close; they did everything together, from tending the few cows, chickens, and goats on the farm to going to minor league baseball games in Albany. Sometimes they drove down to the Big Apple to catch a major league game, when they could afford it.

Those were good, happy times.

But even then, Daniel had to go to the Fulkmaer/GenTech labs several times a year to see Dr. Edwards. He was poked, prodded, and asked a lot of silly questions, never understanding why. Grandpa Jack had given in to these sessions reluctantly. Dr. Edwards told him that the solar radiation which had killed Daniel's parents might have adverse effects on the child as well. They wanted to check his progress periodically . . . or so he said. So Grandpa Jack gave in out of concern for his grandson's life.

After Daniel's grandfather had died, Edwards petitioned the State for custody of the child, citing his concerns for the boy's physical condition. As a medical doctor and geneticist, he was prepared to deal with whatever problems might arise over time, in his opinion. With the help of GenTech's legal staff, Edwards finally secured guardianship of Daniel.

For the last three years, the testing had continued, almost daily. To Daniel, it seemed that Edwards was expecting—even hoping—something would happen, and became frustrated when nothing did. Often Edwards sent the technicians away and worked alone, hooking Daniel up to a variety of machines, sometimes making notes of things that seemed to catch his interest, but usually just giving up angrily.

I guess I know now what the old chromedome was looking for, Daniel thought bitterly. *He was just waiting for something like this to happen. He knew I was a freak.*

Now the late-afternoon sun sifted through the trees, warming the youth's upturned face. *I'll bet it just about fried his gizzard when I cut loose with those blue blasts from my hands and wiped out that wall.*

He could not help but smile at the thought. *And when I shot off like a bottle-rocket—man!*

A shadow passed over the treetops above him, momentarily blocking the rays from the sun. It was accompanied by a muted roar like a small jet.

Daniel sat up with a start. Peering up through the branches, he spotted the source of the noise for an instant, then it disappeared behind the treetops. The roar grew fainter as it moved away from his position.

The black and silver object he had seen was not an airplane, nor any other craft Daniel had ever seen . . . it was a man! It appeared to be armored, but more to the point, it seemed to be searching for something. Daniel could lay odds as to what it was.

I'd better find deeper cover than this, he thought, beginning to rise. The distant thud of car doors slamming came from the direction of the road. Voices drifted into the woods. *They've found me!*

Daniel dropped back down, his temples throbbing with the rapid beating of his heart. *Trapped again!*

Crouching behind the tree, he observed the movements of his enemies.

A metallic-green, four-door sedan, with the emblem of the GenTech Corporation emblazoned in white on the front doors, occupied the roadway next to the field. Six men were standing beside the vehicle, two in dark business suits, the other four in the maroon of the base security unit. One of the business types seemed to be in charge, since he was doing most of the talking and gesturing.

Daniel could not hear what he was saying, but it did not take a genius to know the topic of discussion. Their conference was brief. They quickly divided into two groups of three—one group headed toward the farmhouse; the other made for the barn.

Daniel let out a sigh, not realizing that he had been holding his breath as he strained to hear what they said. Their search pattern would give him an opportunity to move deeper into the woods. Maybe he could find a way to escape without being seen. But the actions of his hunters puzzled him. Why hadn't they sent a team into the woods as well?

His musing was interrupted by a flock of birds suddenly erupting from the treetops northeast of him. *Someone* is *looking for me here! What now?*

More birds were startled from their perches, much nearer this time. No human could move that fast. Did they have dogs after him?

Whatever it was, Daniel did not intend to stand around and find out. He headed off in a westerly direction, trying to be as silent as possible and sticking close to cover. Something crashed through the undergrowth behind him, as if it had caught his scent.

Breaking into a run, Daniel could not bring himself to glance back to see this new menace. Fear dug into him like spurs, urging him on, arms flailing before him to ward off the branches that whipped his face, ignoring the briars that grabbed at his bare legs. He could sense the terror that tracked him—he could hear it coming closer, faster than he could imagine. His breath came in harsh gasps, his chest feeling as if it could explode from fear and lack of air.

Then he went down.

It felt like spiny tentacles had ensnared his right leg, their barbs ripping into his exposed flesh as he lurched forward to the ground. A scream echoed through the trees; Daniel was only vaguely aware that it was his own. He looked back to see what monstrosity had brought him down.

"A bush. A blasted thorn bush!" he hissed through clenched teeth, shaking the sweat from his eyes. Gingerly, he began to pull the thorny branches loose from his damaged leg, expecting his pursuer to come charging in at any second. Then he realized that the sounds of the chase had stopped.

Silence assaulted his ears. Not even the birds could be heard. He sat motionless, listening. Except for the slight swaying of leaves in the breeze, he could detect no movement. For a moment, the stillness seemed almost oppressive to Daniel's shaken nerves, then he began to relax. Perhaps he had somehow lost whoever had been following him. He fell back to the task of extracting his leg from the thorn bush.

"Not much of a hunt," a voice growled behind him. "No matter. The Boss wants you back alive anyway."

Daniel snapped his head around. A tall figure leaned against the bole of an oak, looking rather bored. Apparently, he had been watching the struggling youth for some time. The hope that had built in Daniel's heart melted, leaving an emptiness in his chest that seemed to engulf him.

Grey eyes met his, penetrating him with a malignance that made him shiver. The figure before him was over six feet tall. A mask covered his head, with holes for his eyes and ears, and the lower portion of the man's face was left uncovered, revealing a square jaw. His costume was blue, seemingly one piece, extending from his mask down to the his feet. A dun-colored image of the head and shoulders of a cougar rose up from his waist to the center of his chest. Lithe muscles rippled beneath the skin-tight costume, hard and powerful.

The young fugitive stood up slowly, free from the clinging thorns.

"Dr. Edwards sent you?" he asked.

"Hah! Edwards is a mindless worm," the costumed villain sneered. "The Boss has dozens of flunkies like Edwards working for him. They're expendable."

He grinned as he made a gesture to indicate the termination of one's employment with "the Boss."

"But you're not?" Daniel inquired, looking for a means of escape. *I can't give up now. Grandpa Jack always said that there was no such thing as a problem without a solution. I've just got to find it.*

Glancing at the maze of branches overhead, an idea formed in his mind. He needed to reach a clearing—a pathway to the sky.

The hunter laughed at Daniel's suggestion. "Me? Expendable? Get real, punk. I'm a specialist."

He grinned ominously. "Powered operatives are a rare asset, though what the Boss wants with a runt like you—"

Hoping to catch the man off guard, Daniel darted between the trees as he spoke.

With incredible quickness and agility, the man pounced on him, knocking the wind out of him as they hit the ground. Gripping Daniel by the throat, the villain lifted him up and pinned him against a tree, his feet dangling above the earth.

"No one escapes the Catamount!" the man growled. Daniel could feel the fingers tighten beneath his jaws; air burst from his lips. "I could kill you. But the Boss wouldn't like it."

The pressure was relaxed and Daniel dropped to the ground. Catamount roughly grabbed him by his injured left arm and dragged him back toward the farm.

Daniel hobbled along, wincing with every step, both from the pain in his arm and the wounds to his leg. It felt like the bush had left a few thorns behind.

Paying no heed to Daniel's infirmities, Catamount jerked him along until they exited the woods near the electrified fence.

A shout came from near the car where the six security men had regrouped. Catamount barely acknowledged their call with a curt wave. This was his capture, and no one would share his glory. He led Daniel along the fence toward the road.

This is it, Daniel thought, seeing the open sky above. *If I don't escape now, I may not get another chance.*

His body tensed in anticipation.

Suddenly, a blue glow enveloped him. Catamount reeled back with a howl, grasping his hand as though he had been burned.

Daniel shot into the air. He looked down at his former captor; evidently Catamount was unarmed and could hurl nothing more after him than invectives, which he did freely.

Almost immediately, the reports of small arms fire broke out below him. He could hear the whine of bullets whizzing past, as well as occasional popping sounds as they struck the energy field surrounding his body. There were tiny blue flashes where the bullets connected with the shield, but nothing seemed to penetrate it.

"I'm bulletproof!" Daniel exclaimed. "This light protects me from the shots."

He smiled, a new confidence lighting his features. "Enough of this garbage. It's my turn now."

He dropped into a power-dive, directly toward the antagonists below. Eyes narrowed, he plunged at his target, comet-like discharges leaping from his hands, then he soared back into the sky. The green sedan disintegrated in a blinding explosion, rocking the earth violently, knocking the gunmen off their feet.

"That got their attention." Daniel grinned. It did not look like any of the men had been killed, but they sure were in no hurry to re-engage the young comet.

But Daniel failed to notice the roar of a jet approaching from his left. A burst of heavy machine gun fire scored a direct hit on his protective shield, and he felt a searing burn across his stomach. Several rounds had pierced the shield, though they were still deflected somewhat. Daniel gritted his teeth as his hand touched the shallow crease one had made across his mid-section.

An armored figure sped past him, its trajectory at a right angle to his. Daniel was able to identify his new opponent right away. The black and silver armor with red trim, marked with Nazi swastikas made identification easy. It had been front-page material for the newspapers many times: the Steel Stormtrooper, hero of the neo-Nazi movement, destructive horror to innocent people everywhere.

As the Steel Stormtrooper swung around for a second pass, Daniel decided to attempt a strike of his own. Darting downward at a forty-five degree angle to his foe, he unleashed a blast, certain he would hit the enemy, but the armored villain maneuvered deftly, avoiding the energy bolts. The staccato thunder of the twin machine guns mounted on the right forearm of his armor sent another volley in Daniel's direction.

Daniel dodged awkwardly, almost throwing himself out of control. Again the shield was penetrated, and he could feel the heat of bullets almost brushing his skin. With this near miss came the awareness that he possessed neither the skills nor the agility to do battle with an experienced warrior.

Panic threatened to overwhelm him. *He's going to kill me! I can't fight him—I don't know how.*

He could see the Steel Stormtrooper circling around to come in for the kill. The previous miss had been sheer dumb luck on Daniel's part; there was no guarantee he would survive the next attack.

So, he did the best thing he could think of on short notice: He ran. Some might call it a "strategic withdrawal," but in Daniel's mind he took off like a scared sparrow with a hawk on its tail. He streaked westward, surprised at his own velocity. This was faster than he had ever gone before. Houses and fields and trees flashed by beneath him, blurred by the speed of his passage.

The Steel Stormtrooper dropped far behind. Soon he was out of sight. Apparently, his jet-boots could not achieve the speed that Daniel's energy thrust could. Still, Daniel did not slacken his pace for a while, wanting to be sure his enemy would not catch him.

The sky was entering twilight as Daniel cruised along. The day's events had left him battered and weary. Fatigue set in quickly; the adrenalin of battle drained away, no longer able to sustain him. His left wrist and elbow ached, the slightest movement sent pain stabbing through his arm. His right leg itched and stung almost unbearably from the damage done by the thorns. The flesh wound on his stomach had quit bleeding as far as he could tell, but it still hurt when he stretched the skin at all.

I can't go much further, he thought. *I've got to find a place to land—if I can land without killing myself.*

The memory of his first landing sprang fresh to his mind. *I may fly like a rocket, but I land like a gooney-bird.*

He slowed his airspeed considerably, looking for a place to come down. The terrain was mountainous. It was almost dark now, but it appeared as though the mountains were forested. That made sense; he was probably somewhere over Pennsylvania at this point. The trees should provide seclusion for him during the night, though he did not relish the thought of spending the night outdoors.

Ah, there's as good as place as any, he thought, spying a fairly large clearing. It had what appeared to be an abandoned brick building in the center of it, with a gravel road running away from the front of the structure. There was room for him to land, whatever his method might be.

Here goes nothing. Resisting the temptation to close his eyes as he neared the grassy clearing, he willed his body to slow. The light surrounding him dimmed, but did not go out. It was hard to judge distances in the dark. When he felt he was close enough, he tried to lessen his energy output and swung his feet toward the ground.

He hit hard. His injured leg buckled beneath him and he tumbled forward several feet. When he came to rest, he sat up, groggy from both the impact and fatigue.

Well, it's a step in the right direction, he thought wryly. *At least I didn't come in like a kamikaze this time. Maybe I'll get the hang of this yet.*

Further inspection verified that the building was indeed empty. He could not determine its purpose. It was evident by the oil stains and mountings on the cement floor that it had once housed heavy machinery, but Daniel could not guess their function. A few packing crates and tattered tarpaulins lay scattered about the floor, and remnants of workbenches and scrap metal lined the walls. Chunks of concrete and wooden beams cluttered one end of the workshop.

The second story of the building was really not a story at all. It consisted of a wide balcony, which housed several small, open offices. The center of the building was open to the ceiling, part of which had collapsed at some time, obviously the source of the debris at the end of the room.

Daniel limped over to one of the oily tarpaulins. He shook the dust from it and slung it over his shoulder. Finding a second tarp, he rolled it into a bundle and set it on the floor by one of the workbenches. The wound on his stomach was still wet, so he located a torn place on the first tarp, finished tearing it off, and wrapped it around his middle. Then he lay down on the cold cement and pulled the remainder of the cloth over him like a blanket.

He shivered from the touch of the chill floor against his bare back. A stabbing hurt shot through his torso as he attempted to curl up for warmth. Groaning, he straightened out again, pulling his cover up to his chin and crossing his right arm over his chest; his swollen left arm rested against his leg. Exhausted and hurting as he was, sleep still did not come easily.

A tear formed in the corner of his eye as he stared at the ceiling high above. It trickled down his cheek, splashing against his shoulder before it found the floor. The hopelessness of his situation crushed his mind. He knew he had only found a temporary shelter. Eventually, he would have to go back out in the open again, and become a moving target once more.

Where can I go? Grandpa Jack, I don't know the solution to this problem. I need you, Grandpa; I can't make it on my own. A tremor rippled through the boy's face. *There's no one I can turn to. Who would take in a—a freak. Nobody cares anymore. Nobody.*

The tears flowed more freely now; he did not attempt to wipe them away. After all, there was no one to see them.

* * * *

His fitful sleep was fraught with images of mad scientists and laboratories, of soaring through the clouds with the birds. Then a forest where he fled in slow motion from an unseen predator, knowing a horrible death awaited him if he were caught. Long, hideous tendrils reached for him, poison dripping from their thorns as they burned into his flesh. A black shape thundered toward him from a darkened sky, flame spouting from its hands.

Daniel awakened with a jerk, the roar of the jets still echoing in his ears. He wiped the perspiration from his face. The sun glared through the first story windows in the east, illuminating the interior of the building, vacant except for one lone and battered occupant.

Moaning with the effort, Daniel struggled to his feet, wrapping the tarpaulin around his shoulders to ward off the early morning chill. He was terribly thirsty, but soon discovered that there was no running water in the place. Evidently it had been turned off when the building had been abandoned. He decided to go outside to see if he could find a creek, a puddle, anything.

Crossing the room to the entrance, he reached for the knob. Suddenly, the door crashed from its hinges, smashing the youth head on and coming down on top of him as he hit the cement floor.

A black, metallic boot landed on the door, crushing the wind out of him. "You embarrassed me, freak. No Genate scum does that to me!"

The dark visor of the Steel Stormtrooper's helmet hovered over the prone boy menacingly. "Now you'll pay for it. Contract or no contract, you're gonna die."

The Stormtrooper's gauntlet wrenched him out from under the door, the tarp still clinging to the boy's body. Ripping the cover away, he flung Daniel into the workbenches against the wall.

Daniel slid to the floor, stunned. He tried vainly to get up, but the enemy's palm thudded against his sternum, sending him sliding across the rubble-strewn floor. If he could just get a shot off. . . .

But it was not to be. Before he could rouse himself, the Steel Stormtrooper's boot smashed into his side. Daniel felt ribs crack with the impact.

He's just playing with me, he thought, breathing heavily, vision dimmed by the pain. *He can kill me any time he wants.*

The assassin lifted him by the shoulders. "Your kind is the pollution of humanity, freak. You gotta be taught a lesson, then you gotta die."

With one hand, he threw Daniel toward the wall again.

Crashing through a window, Daniel felt himself sailing through the air, shards of glass clinging in his hair. There was a sharp grinding in his side as he struck the ground. It took every ounce of strength he had left to rise to his knees.

The Steel Stormtrooper laughed as he stalked toward the youth. "You're nothing, freak. I could snap you like a twig."

As Daniel labored to regain his feet, an armored fist struck him full in the face. He sprawled backwards into the damp grass. Head ringing, he could taste blood in his mouth. There was no energy left in him; he was finished.

A thick, bare leg stepped over him, obscuring his view of all but the armored boots of the Steel Stormtrooper.

There was a heavy metallic *bong*, and Daniel saw his opponent flying on a flat trajectory toward the brick wall forty feet away. The Stormtrooper crashed through the bricks, disappearing from sight.

Through the fog in his mind, Daniel could discern a massive figure striding forward, placing himself between the building and the boy. When the figure turned to look back at him, he could see that it was a giant of a man—at least seven and a half feet tall, thickly muscled, with biceps as big around as Daniel's waist.

He wore a light blue mask, with a matching costume which left his arms bare, and ended in shorts with his legs exposed as well. A yellow crown was pictured on the forehead of the mask, and a circle with three matching crowns arranged in an upside-down triangle adorned his chest. Light blue boots completed the outfit.

Daniel blinked against the haze before his eyes, not quite believing what he was seeing. According to news reports he had seen, the man defending him was a member of the Champions of Justice, a hero team based out of Philadelphia.

A machine gun burst erupted from the hole made by the Steel Stormtrooper's body. The giant did not even flinch as the rounds ricocheted off his immense chest. The Stormtrooper raised his left arm, the forearm of which contained what looked like a small rocket-launcher. Flame spurted from the dark opening, and streaked toward the rescuer. The rocket exploded against the giant's torso. He rocked back slightly, steadying himself with his hands.

A baritone voice, tinged with a Swedish accent, challenged the armored villain, "Come, vermin . . . feel the might of the Swede."

"This isn't your fight, musclehead," the villain answered, fingering the dent in his breast-plate made by the powerful hero. "Why don't you butt out before I have to hurt you."

The Swede smiled grimly. "You come on ahead, if you dare to . . . or do you only hit children? Nazi coward!"

With an enraged cry, the Steel Stormtrooper launched himself into the air, jets blazing, directly at the towering Swede.

A huge hand swung forward to meet the onslaught, catching the armored criminal by the helmet. As Daniel watched, his head swimming in a dark mist, the Swede bent his opponent backward between his mighty paws, until Daniel thought the villain would snap. Then the Swede pounded the Steel Stormtrooper against a nearby tree; the Nazi ceased to move.

"If you harm children, you must answer to me," the Swede muttered angrily. Turning away from his subdued opponent, he walked over to where the youth still lay only half-conscious.

Daniel felt two massive hands slide under him, and was tenderly lifted off the ground as if he were light as a feather.

"No more worries, boy. Hold on, no one can hurt you now. Help is coming." The Swede's words echoed in Daniel's mind as he slipped into unconsciousness.

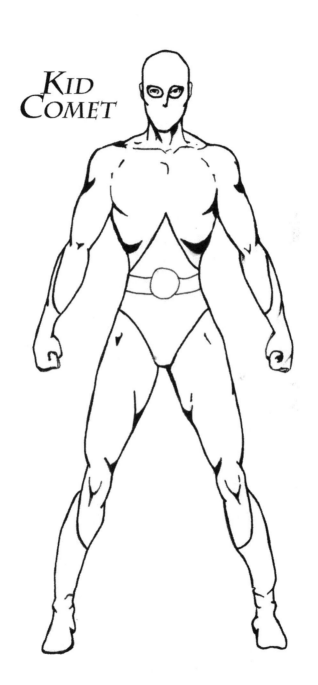

Speedette:
At Her Own Speed

by

Becca Lynn Rudder

A young girl, about sixteen, crept silently into the room. Not much could be seen in the dark, pierced only by one small light source—a Scooby-Doo nightlight—but she still found what she was looking for . . . a giant-size adventure comic. She picked it up carefully, checked to see that the comic book's owner was still asleep, and made her way soundlessly from the room.

"Phew, got it!" she said to herself upon reaching safety. "And Mom didn't even catch me this time!"

"You were saying?"

The girl sheepishly turned toward her mother.

"Ah . . . nothing. I didn't say anything," she replied with a grin, hiding the comic book behind her back.

Her mother rolled her eyes. "I know you took one of little Jimmy's comic books again, Kelcie."

She shook her head. "How many times do I have to tell you not to?"

Kelcie gave a long, drawn out sigh. "But *Mom* . . . Jimmy never *lets* me read them. I ask . . . I *do!* He always says no! So, what else am I supposed to do?"

Mrs. Pryce looked at her daughter sternly for a moment, then broke into laughter. "Kelcie, he's only seven. He's just started reading more than little kid books. He loves being able to read those comic books by himself, and you're just aggravating him more and more by constantly sneaking off with them."

"Only one at a time," Kelcie pointed out, trying to look innocent. "He doesn't need to act like I'm . . . I don't know, trying to take his Easter candy or something."

Mrs. Pryce smiled. "I know. I'm trying to work with him on that. But you're still not helping when you take them anyway after he's said no."

"I guess you're right, but still, can't I just go ahead and read *this* one, since I've already got it *anyway*?" Kelcie pleaded, holding the comic book out in front of her and looking up at her mother with big blue eyes.

Mrs. Pryce stared at her for a moment, then sighed. "Fine . . . but no more. Do you understand me, Kelcie Olivia Pryce?"

Kelcie grinned. "Yes, ma'am. Thanks!"

After her mother left the room, Kelcie closed her bedroom door. She put on her Lady Speed pajamas, turned on the lamp beside her bed, then turned off the overhead light. She climbed into bed and opened her brother's comic book.

* * * *

"Kelcie!" came an outraged little voice.

Kelcie blinked, then glanced at her window. Light was coming through the curtains. She had not gotten to the third page of the comic book before falling asleep. Now, she would have to give it back to Jimmy, and she barely knew how it even started!

Or would she?

"Ah . . . yes, Jimmy?" she called back, hiding the comic book under her pillow. She threw on her Emerald Avenger robe before opening the door.

A seven-year-old boy with blue-green eyes that glinted with suspicion stood there with his little fists clenched at his sides. His flaming red cheeks matched his hair. In his over-sized Camo-lad robe and little teddy bear slippers, he looked rather adorable . . . except to his sister, who was trying not to look or sound guilty.

"You took my *Magnificent Protectors* book again, didn't you?" Jimmy said, pointing an accusing finger at her.

"*What*? Why would I do a thing like that? And, it's a *comic* book, Jimmy. Books are different."

"You know what I mean, Kelcie! And I know why you would, too, so did you or not?"

"Maybe I did, and maybe I didn't," Kelcie replied mysteriously, then she grinned. "See you downstairs!"

She closed the door in his face, latching it, so she could get ready for school.

In a short time, Kelcie was dressed, had her bookbag packed, and had made her way down to the kitchen to enjoy a blueberry muffin breakfast . . . enjoying it as much as she could with her little brother giving her the evil eye as he gobbled down his own food. As soon as she could, she finished and grabbed her bag to head off to school.

"Kelcie, the bus isn't here yet," her father said with a frown. "Where are you going?"

"Ah . . . school's not *that* far, Dad, and I . . . need my exercise? Bye!"

With that, she was off.

Twenty minutes later, Kelcie walked through the big double doors at the main entrance to Petra County High School—starting to wish she had waited for the bus. She went over to her locker and struggled with the combination. She could never remember which one had been her middle school combination and which was her current one. She almost always tried the wrong combination first.

Another sixteen-year-old girl walked up to her, grinning. "A sophomore now and still can't remember, huh?"

Kelcie rolled her eyes, then tried the other combination. It worked like a charm.

"Thank you, Lacey," she said with a sigh.

"No problem!" Lacey replied, still grinning. "Anything new with you?"

"Oh, nothing much. I think I'm failing geometry, Dad's heading out to Reading for a conference of some sort in about a week, and I took another one of Jimmy's comic books. You know, the usual."

"Kelcie, I thought your mom told you 'no more'—repeatedly," Lacey said with a frown.

"I know, but . . . I don't know, Lace. I just really want to read them."

"Couldn't you get your own?"

Kelcie's hand hovered over the Spanish textbook she had been reaching for. "Yes, I guess I could. But why have more than one copy of the exact same thing in the house? It's not like it's a china set . . . it's a *comic book!*"

Lacey nodded slightly, golden hair shimmering a bit in the fluorescent lighting. "Well, yeah, but . . . still. Pretty soon Jimmy's *going* to get back at you, and I'm pretty sure you're going to like whatever he does about as much as he likes you taking his comics."

"I know," Kelcie sighed. "I'll figure all that out later, though—time for English. You coming or what?"

Lacey giggled. "Yeah, I'm coming . . . except that we're headed to Spanish, remember?"

Kelcie frowned, finally grabbing the book she had gone for out of the locker and staring at it. "Oh, right. Talk about a blonde moment!"

"Hey!" Lacey said, flipping one of her own golden locks and looking mock-insulted.

Kelcie grinned. "Hehe, sorry."

The two shared a laugh, then headed to class.

About three hours later, Kelcie and Lacey sat down in the cafeteria to a Taco Tuesday lunch. Kelcie only picked at her taco, sighing to herself.

"What's wrong, Kelce?" Lacey asked, concern in her face and voice.

"Oh, just that I was right—I *am* failing geometry. I got a fifty-three on yesterday's quiz."

Lacey gasped. "Kelcie! I told you I would help you with it, if you wanted me to."

Kelcie laughed mirthlessly.

"I wasn't going to cheat on the quiz, Lace," she admonished her best friend.

Lacey rolled her eyes. "You're no fun."

"Lacey!"

The girl giggled. "I'm kidding, Kelce, I'm kidding. You take things way too seriously."

Kelcie smiled sheepishly. "I know, I know. Sorry."

Lacey shook her head. "Don't worry about it. What you *do* need to worry about is getting those grades up. Didn't your father say you had to pass all your classes if you wanted to get your driver's permit this year?"

Kelcie sagged in her seat. "Yes, he did. I'm *trying*. I just can't seem to wrap my mind around dumb old geometry."

Lacey snapped her fingers. "What you need is a tutor! Or, I don't know, your mother?"

She rolled her eyes once more. "You *do* remember that she's a teacher, right?"

"Yeah, at the *elementary* school! They don't have to take geometry!"

"Maybe not, but still . . . didn't your mom have to take geometry when *she* was in high school? Probably took some quizzes herself, not *just* in high school, but to get her teacher's license, too."

"Huh," Kelcie said thoughtfully. "You're probably right. Guess I'd better ask her."

"You think?" Lacey sighed. "There's the bell. Come on, let's get to history."

Kelcie nodded as she grabbed her book-bag, and followed Lacey down the hallway back to their classroom. She never could remember what the lesson was that day—which showed a bit on her next report card. She was out of it, distracted by the fact that she might have to wait another year to get her driver's permit . . . and how much she positively *hated* geometry.

The rest of the day came and went. A few short hours later, Kelcie stepped off the bus and walked through her front door. She went up to her room to start on her homework, getting everything out of the way fairly quickly . . . except for geometry and that day's history. She muddled through the latter, then simply glared at the former for the better part of five minutes before she was interrupted by a soft knock at her door.

"Kelcie, supper in about ten minutes. Come on down!" her mother called.

"Ah . . . all right, Mom!" Kelcie replied, setting aside the subject of her doom.

After another grueling meal under the accusatory glare of her seven-year-old brother, she tackled villainous old Geometry.

* * * *

Two weeks and a terrible geometry score later—not having taken Lacey's advice to have her mother help her—Kelcie stepped off the bus and climbed the stairs to the main school building. She half-heartedly tried first one and then the other of her locker combinations and sifted through her cluttered locker for her chemistry goggles. There was going to be a special extended experiment that day that would cover class time until lunch break.

Kelcie was not really thrilled about it. She usually loved chemistry—and wanted to keep working on it after class was over—but today, all she could think about was the fact that her father had told her no driving for another year. She was over three-quarters of the way through the school year now; there was no way she could make up her geometry enough to pass it.

She would have to suffer through it again the next year.

Kelcie blinked as she felt herself being shaken from behind.

"L-Lacey...!" she exclaimed, jerking out of her best friend's grasp.

"Ah, so the dilapidated Miss Pryce does live! She's not just a mournful statue!" Lacey remarked sarcastically.

"The dila... what?"

Lacey rolled her eyes. "*You're* supposed to be the smart one, and I know a word you don't? You're falling down on the job, Kelce."

Kelcie just glared at her and slipped her goggles on. "Ha-ha, you're so funny."

Lacey shook her head. "I'm not the one who said you can't drive. I'm not going to be driving yet either. No need to be mad at me for trying to bring you back to Earth from the Dumpsville."

She popped open her locker and grabbed her own goggles.

Kelcie sighed and tried to smile. "I know... I'm sorry. Just need to accept it and move on."

She straightened up and grabbed her friend by the arm. "Come on, partner—onward to the lab!"

With a matched set of giggles, they made their way to class.

* * * *

Once everyone had donned their lab coats and seated themselves at their respective stations, Mr. Lochness—not to be confused with the mythical monster—began to speak in his big, booming, bass voice.

"Before each of you is a beaker. In the beaker is a bluish-purple liquid. Who can tell me what chemical is in this beaker?"

Kelly Ryles, the class show-off, lifted her nose into the air and said—so smugly that Kelcie wanted to smack her—"Tri-xenon dimethylate, of course."

Her smug look turned to that of a wet puppy when Mr. Lochness' voice dropped at least an octave—a feat Kelcie did not even think was possible—and said, "Wrong."

A triumphant laugh rippled through the class until Mr. Lochness stood to his full six-feet-eight-inches and *glared* at them. Upon seeing his stormy mountain transformation, Kelcie—and everyone else—knew it was time to shut up and listen.

Mr. Lochness gave a quick nod and resumed his seat. "That's better. Now, does anyone else wish to venture a guess?"

Lacey lifted her hand high and waved it around.

"Pick me, pick me, pick me," she murmured under her breath.

Kelcie could not believe Lacey actually wanted to put forth a guess. She usually just supported whatever Kelcie's answer was.

Mr. Lochness seemed surprised as well, but nodded to her. "Yes, Miss Dumont?"

Lacey took a breath, then proudly stated, "It's only *one* element, not a compound!"

Mr. Lochness nodded again slowly. "Yes, that's true . . . but what *is* the element?"

Lacey looked at Kelcie, then back to Mr. Lochness and shrugged. "I don't know."

Mr. Lochness barely stifled a laugh.

"That makes a little more sense," he said quietly, as though he thought the students could not hear him.

Kelcie, however, did, and put her hand over her mouth to hide a giggle of her own.

Mr. Lochness cleared his throat. "Yes, well . . . it is a newly-discovered element. Who knows what that element is?"

Kelcie watched as Ronald Riker slowly raised his hand. He was sort of shy, but she still thought he was *so* cute!

"Yes, Mr. Riker?" Mr. Lochness acknowledged him.

Ronald hesitated, glancing around at all the eyes fixed on him, then looked straight at the teacher and said, "That would b-be merenthium, S-Sir."

Kelcie, in true teen-aged girliness, thought that she would cherish that element name forever.

"Merenthium," she repeated to herself dreamily.

Lacey gave her a good jab in the ribs.

"Pay attention to Teach, not Ronnie," she admonished, though the amused look on her face gave indication that she thought her best friend was being adorable—or perhaps more accurately, a*dork*able.

Kelcie was oblivious to the look. "He prefers Ronald. . . ."

Lacey sighed, then grabbed her friend's head and turned it from Ronald to Mr. Lochness.

The latter shook his head once in their direction, then smiled at Ronald. "That is correct, Mr. Riker. The element before you is merenthium, and this is the first time a high school has been allowed to conduct experiments using it."

"Wait a minute," Lacey said, eyes going wide. "Petra High is the very first school to use it?"

"Yes, Miss Dumont. Kindly raise your hand when you have a question."

"Score!" Lacey shouted.

"Miss Dumont. . . ."

"That wasn't a question," she muttered to herself before shutting her mouth.

Kelcie gave her friend a pat on the arm, then listened eagerly to Mr. Lochness.

"Merenthium has been found in basic studies to aid in the decomposition of many chemical compounds," he said. "Especially hydrochloric acid, citric acid, and even more commonplace compounds like iron oxide and water.

"Your first experiment, class, is to find the correct amount of merenthium to completely decompose water into its component elements—two atoms of hydrogen and one of oxygen per molecule. Does everyone have a beaker of water at their station?"

A military-like "Sir, yes Sir!" resounded throughout the classroom. Everyone was excited about this assignment—especially Kelcie—and they could not wait to get started.

* * * *

Two or three hours passed, and Kelcie had successfully decomposed three of the four compounds Mr. Lochness had assigned for the experiment: iron oxide, citric acid, and—of course—the water. Hydrochloric acid was proving to be much more of a challenge, which she had expected. She had only succeeded in decomposing it about a quarter of the way and had taken her gloves off to turn a page in her notebook, when she heard Lacey give a quiet cheer beside her.

"You're done already?" she whispered, eyes goggling in disbelief.

"Yeah," Lacey whispered back, a little bit louder than Kelcie. "Finally got that water divided up! What do I do now?"

Kelcie found it hard to bite back a laugh. For someone who was surprisingly skilled in arithmetic, Lacey seemed to barely comprehend chemistry.

A snarky voice announced the sudden presence of Kelly Ryles by their station. "You blockhead! I finished the *whole* assignment, like, so half an hour ago, and you *just* finished the *first* thing? Pa- and -thetic, Dumy."

She always talked like the stereotypical 'popular girl,' though she was anything but popular. Kelcie just thought she sounded like a whackadoo.

Kelcie felt anger starting to warm her face. "Hey, leave Lacey alone, Ryles."

Kelly rolled her eyes. "Yeah, right. What*ever!*"

"Just let it go, Kelce," Lacey said. "Don't need to make a scene in class, do we?"

Kelcie was shocked to hear these words come out of Lacey's mouth, but she heeded them. She completely ignored Kelly's existence beside them and began writing down her notes.

Kelly huffed and whipped around to make a dramatic exit, managing to smack into the rack of chemicals on the station, knocking it over. More than two dozen different chemicals and compounds spilled over Kelcie's notes—and her bare hands—in the process.

The rack also collided with the beaker of merenthium, shattering it and dousing Kelcie's hands. Kelcie screamed, jerking her hands away from the counter and trying to shake the chemicals off of them. "*Kelly!*"

Kelly paid no attention to her, chatting with a fellow 'popular girl' about how lame Kelcie and Lacey were, as seemed to be her ultimate pleasure in life.

Kelcie stared down at her hands . . . they were *glowing*. Her eyes widened. Blue and sparkling—yes, her hands *were* glowing! She held them stock-still—or, rather, scared stiff—below the edge of the counter.

After a few seconds more, the glittering light suddenly streamed up her arms, beneath her sleeves, and was gone.

"Kelce! Are you all right?"

She blinked as Lacey shook her shoulder again, face full of concern. "I . . . I, umm . . . think I'd better go to the nurse."

Mr. Lochness' booming voice startled her from behind.

"Nurse? No. I already called 911; an ambulance is on its way. You're headed to the hospital, Miss Pryce!" he declared, grabbing her arm and rushing her over to the lab's water station. "Most of those chemicals—especially the merenthium—are dangerously apt to burn your hands. I warned all of you about that!"

Kelcie reddened. "I know, Mr. Lochness. I *was* being careful."

Mr. Lochness looked at her ungloved, dripping hands, and Kelcie stopped talking. That was on her, even if Ryles did knock the chemicals down. She knew she should not have let Kelly get under her skin. If she had remained focused, she might have remembered to put her gloves back on after turning the page.

After the mandatory, twenty-minute flushing of her hands in the emergency water station, Kelcie sighed as an EMT herded her to the ambulance.

"But I feel fine. Look, no burns!" She held up her hands for inspection. She hesitated to mention the brief glow . . . or the weird, warm, fuzzy feeling flowing inside her.

Even noting the peculiar absence of burn marks, Mr. Lochness ordered the EMT to rush Kelcie to the hospital. She was not sure if he thought there might be delayed reaction burns, but she was not really eager to have some doctor inspecting her for possible side effects anyway. She had never liked doctors. They liked to stick her with pointy needles. Sure, her mom said those were *vaccinations* and *immunizations*, but Kelcie just knew they were out to get her.

Before she knew it, Kelcie was being wheeled into Petra County General on a gurney, much to her disdain. She told them over and over on the whole ten-minute ambulance ride there that she felt fine and could walk in on her own. The EMTs would not listen to her; they just followed protocol, and Petra protocol was "if it's bad enough to rush to the hospital for, put 'em on a gurney." Or at least that was what Kelcie was thinking as they rolled her into the room.

The EMTs carefully moved her from gurney to bed and told her that Dr. West would be in shortly. As soon as they left, Kelcie sat up on the edge of the bed, feeling rather nervous.

A jumble of questions raced through her mind. What *was* happening to her, after all? Would this Dr. West, whoever he was, be able to figure it out? How many chemicals had mixed together with that merenthium, and why did she feel so funny *all over* when she had only got the mixture on her hands? And why did she glow?

Pondering these questions, she did not notice when Dr. West entered the room; rather, she was facing the door when it opened and a white coat appeared. She heard the door close again. After a moment, her eyes focused on the coat, and she brought her gaze up to the owner's face.

Dr. West was not a he. She was a she—and looked much too young to be a doctor.

The doctor laughed faintly at the wide-eyed look on Kelcie's face, then dipped her head to her. "Hello,

Miss"—she consulted her clipboard—"Miss Pryce. What seems to be the trouble today?"

Kelcie blinked. This doctor with mousey brown hair and a cordial smile was holding a clipboard that apparently had her information on it. She should already know why she was here.

Kelcie sighed, then held up her hands. "A rack of chemicals came crashing down on my station at school and spilled all over my hands."

"Including the new merenthium, yes?" Dr. West appeared to be jotting down some notes.

Kelcie nodded slowly. *Seriously?* she thought.

It was all too obviously already on the paper. Why was she writing the same thing down again?

"Wait . . . what?" Kelcie murmured to herself as these twisting, mixed-up thoughts rolled around in her head.

Dr. West looked up from her notes. "What was that, Miss Pryce? Or may I call you Kelcie?"

Kelcie shook her head. "Sorry, nothing. Umm, I guess you could . . . if you tell me your first name, Dr. West."

If she had to be here, she at least wanted to know who she was dealing with.

Dr. West laughed once again. "Fair enough."

She slipped on a pair of latex gloves as she answered, "I'm Penelope West. You can call me Dr. West, or Dr. Penelope, or even Doc Penny, if you think it would sound cooler."

This last part was obviously designed to break down Kelcie's walls and make her laugh. It definitely worked.

"Doc Penny?" she said between giggles. "I think I like Dr. Penelope best."

Dr. Penelope smiled. "Well, then, you just call me that. Now, let's get a look at these hands of yours," she said, taking one by the wrist and moving it around carefully, following suit with the other. "I certainly don't see any burning. Curious."

She picked up her clipboard and studied the notes on it. "I have an inventory of which chemicals were on your counter, and almost all of them should have burned you to one degree or another. The merenthium alone could have nearly melted them off. I still don't condone it being studied in high schools. So dangerous. . . ."

Her voice trailed off as she considered what the next step should be.

Kelcie's eyes bugged wildly as she stared back and forth between Dr. Penelope and her hands.

"M-melted off?" she stammered in shock.

Dr. Penelope's countenance took on a shocked expression of her own. Apparently she had not meant to say that part out loud. "Well, umm . . . this is why we wear gloves during our experiments and *keep them on*, yes?"

Kelcie was sure all the color had drained from her face by now as she stared unbelievingly at Dr. Penelope.

The doctor put a hand on her shoulder. "Now, don't fret; if it was going to burn you, it would have done so by now. Still, I am going to have to call your parents to see if I can get a few tests done on you."

Kelcie nodded her head emphatically.

"Call them right now, please!" she replied. Burned-off-hands fear took precedence over hospital fear any day of the week. She wanted to be checked out right away.

Dr. Penelope smiled kindly at her and went to the door. After a moment, she flagged down a passing orderly. "Tell Nurse Cheryl to call the parents of Miss Kelcie Pryce back, would you? I need their per—"

"Our what? Anything! Where's my little girl?" Kelcie heard her mother's frantic voice outside the door.

Her father was only slightly more composed. "Anything you need to do, Doctor, do it. Just . . . can we see her first?"

Jimmy was bawling. Kelcie wondered if the whole hospital could hear the little silly-willy from that hallway.

Dr. Penelope backed back into the room, nodding. "Yes, you can see her for a few minutes while I set up the tests. Please don't faint, Mrs. Pryce—it's just routine."

With that, Kelcie's family entered the room, her father supporting her distraught mother and dragging little Jimmy, who was clinging to his leg. Thankfully, none of her classmates were sitting out there. She felt downright ridiculous.

"Oh, Kelcie. . . !"

She held up her hand. "Mom, before you start blubbering like Baby J here"—this nickname got her a glare from her little brother—"just look and listen."

She waved her hands out in front of her. "See, didn't melt off or anything."

Mrs. Pryce looked like her eyes were going to pop clear out of her head. "They could have done that?!"

Kelcie ran a hand down her face. Did she really have to mention that possibility to her mother? "The important thing is, they didn't."

"Then why does that Doctor . . . Doctor. . . ."

"Penelope West," Kelcie supplied.

"Yes, well, why does she need to do tests if you're fine?"

"I didn't say that, Mom."

"What?"

"No . . . I mean . . . well . . . *she* didn't say that, either. She needs to do tests to make sure nothing's wrong that's not readily visible, I guess. But, Mom . . . Mom . . . *Mom!* Good grief. . . ."

This time, Kelcie did a double face-palm as her mother broke down into a complete hysteria. "Did you not just hear her say the word *routine*? She doesn't seem to think there will really be anything wrong—"

"Unless she's really good at hiding things from you!"

Kelcie grinned. "Believe me, I don't think that's the case . . . *at all*."

Mr. Pryce gently shook his wife once or twice. "Madeline, settle down before you give yourself a stroke. I'm sure that Doctor. . . ."

"West," Kelcie said, a little annoyed.

"Dr. West knows what she's doing, Madeline. If she thinks there's a problem, she'll tell us. If she doesn't know until the tests are completed, hon, that's only normal. Like Kelcie said, nothing's visible on the outside, but they need to make sure nothing's wrong on the inside."

Mrs. Pryce wiped the tears from her eyes with a sigh. "I know, I know . . . but she's our *baby*, Cliff!"

"Wait a minute!" a high-pitched little voice entered the mix. "I thought *I* was the baby!"

Kelcie looked Jimmy square in the eye. "Oh, now you *want* to be called the baby?"

He tilted his head with a confused little look on his face, then shook his head. "No, I don't want to be *called* it. I just thought that was *my* title, not yours."

He gave a little shrug.

Kelcie giggled at her dorky little brother, and soon father and even hysterical mother could not help laughing at the offended look on the seven-year-old boy's face.

Dr. Penelope returned just at that moment with a second clipboard and a jovial smile. "Well, it's nice to hear laughter pouring out into the hallway. Most of the time we don't hear much of that down here."

She held out the new clipboard and a pen. "Now, if you'll just sign—"

Mrs. Pryce grabbed the clipboard, quickly scrawled her name on the paper, and handed it back to the doctor. "There, now do whatever you have to do!"

Dr. Penelope looked at her strangely, then down at the clipboard.

"Well, umm . . . *Mr.* Pryce," she said, stepping away from Mrs. Pryce and turning toward him. "Now that your wife has . . . signed"—she cleared her throat—"the blank entitled 'name of insurance provider,' if you would kindly place *your* signature on the 'owner of insurance policy' line and fill out the permission information for your daughter to undergo medical procedures, that would be very helpful. Then we can begin as soon as possible and *get her home* as soon as possible."

Mrs. Pryce turned several shades of red as her husband filled out these portions of the paper.

Dr. Penelope looked it over once he was finished. "There, now I can begin the tests. You will need to fill out the rest of the information—"

"Including the *actual* insurance provider, seeing that isn't Mom," Kelcie threw in.

Everyone shared a laugh at that—except Jimmy, who was not exactly sure why everyone was laughing—and Dr. Penelope nodded. "Yes, including that. Please hand the paperwork over to Nurse Cheryl at the Number Two Nurse's Station in the atrium when you are finished."

"Will do," Kelcie's father said with a nod.

Dr. Penelope nodded in return. "Well, then, everyone say a quick good-bye to Kelcie so we can get to work."

Jimmy looked up at her. "She gonna be all right?"

Dr. Penelope smiled gently at him. "Don't worry. She'll be ok."

Jimmy did not look convinced, but simply shrugged once more and turned to look at his sister again.

Mrs. Pryce, who had finally calmed down, turned toward her daughter.

"All right then," she pulled her into a hug. "Love you, Kelcie."

"Me, too, little one," her father added gently, giving her shoulder a squeeze.

"You'll be all right, Kelcie," Jimmy assured her, still sounding very unconvinced and *un*-reassuring.

Kelcie shook her head at them with a smile. "I love you all, too, and I'm sure I will, Jim-Jim."

"Don't call me that, Kelcie!"

With one last laugh together—even shared by Jimmy, after a few seconds of being miffed—Kelcie's family was ushered out the door, and it was just Kelcie and Dr. Penelope West once again.

The blood work went quickly and smoothly, and Dr. Penelope left the room momentarily to get it down to the lab.

Kelcie looked around the room, wondering what else the doctor was going to do to her, when all of a sudden that warm, fuzzy feeling ran through her again. She jerked and looked down at her hands. Once again, they glowed blue and the light ran completely over her. Only this time it was more pronounced, not so faint.

What's going on? she wondered.

* * * *

Because they were dealing with a new chemical substance, Dr. Penelope recommended that Kelcie stay at the hospital overnight for observation. In the morning, Kelcie's parents picked her up and brought her home.

She went up to her room, threw on some clean clothes, and skipped back down the stairs to the sound of sizzling bacon. She felt just fine today, and even though she had experienced more blue surges while she was at the hospital—curiously only when Dr. Penelope was not looking at her or in the room—she was all packed up, ready to head for school.

She slipped one strap of her book-bag over the back of a kitchen chair before sitting down, then looked around at her parents and brother—wondering why each one of them was staring at her with such weird looks on their faces.

She glanced down for a second, thinking she might have accidently put on a stained shirt or ripped jeans, but her clothing looked just fine to her. She started to feel her hair.

"Did I forget to brush it out or something?" she asked, though it did not feel that way.

"Umm . . . no, sweetie. We just didn't expect. . . ." Her mother's voice trailed off.

Kelcie let out a laugh as realization hit her. She patted her backpack. "Expect me to go to school today? Is that it? Guys, I'm *fine*."

Her father shook his head. "The test results aren't supposed to be in until Saturday, Kelcie . . . I think everyone is just expecting you *not* to be back until next week, that's all."

Kelcie's eyes widened. "Uh huh. As in, the school called to make sure the Chem Kid doesn't contaminate the whole student body and faculty and anyone else who might be there."

She stood straight up out of her chair and shoved it into the table. "If I *was* poisonous, or . . . or . . . contagious, or something, they wouldn't have sent me home to infect *you* with it, would they?"

Mrs. Pryce put her hand on her daughter's shoulder. "Of course not, Kelcie. It's just a . . . precaution."

Kelcie was taken aback by that statement. "Oh, yeah? Is that so?"

She grabbed her backpack and slung it over her shoulder. "If they wanted to take a 'precaution,' they could've just, I don't know, made me wear gloves or something the whole time until Saturday. But Dr. Penelope didn't seem to think that was necessary, did she? Good grief. . . ."

She ended in a mutter, stomping back up the stairs to her room.

"Kelcie!" Mr. Pryce called after her, but she just finished climbing the stairs and slammed her bedroom door.

"Why?" she growled at her bed as she threw her backpack down as hard as she could onto it. "I'm *fine*!"

She jerked slightly as another unexpected fuzzy wave lanced through her body, another, brighter blue shimmer running all over her. It did not hurt, it just freaked her out every time it happened . . . and that was happening more frequently.

"Except for that, I suppose," she murmured, opening the notebook on her desk. She had made marks in it for each time she had surged. "Tenth time, unless it happened while I was asleep last night."

She shook her head. "That would have woke me up—probably. What *is* it, though?"

Off and on, when no one else was around, she would think about telling someone, but every time she had the opportunity, she was afraid to say anything. She rationalized that it was just the confusion of it all. Maybe she would tell Dr. Penelope when they went to see her again on Saturday.

"Sure, why not?" she muttered to herself, slumping onto the edge of her bed.

"And, in the meantime, I get to stay home from school instead of letting everybody know that, really, I'm okay! *Su*per-*du*per!" she finished sarcastically, flinging herself backward on her bed and staring up at the ceiling. "Yay, me. . . ."

* * * *

Kelcie continued her pout until early that evening, having gone through surges eleven through fifteen in the eight-hour interim since breakfast. She had really planned to stay in her room until the next day, but her room did not have any source of food in it, and, for some reason, she was starving. She felt like she had not eaten anything since yesterday . . . which was true.

She took a breath and slowly opened the door. She still was not thrilled about her parents going along with the school's and doctor's wishes for her to stay home from school until Monday, but she was getting tired of being mad about it.

"There's my little girl," Mr. Pryce said with a smile.

Kelcie did not look up at him. "Hey, Dad."

"Kelcie, look at me." Her father waited until she did before continuing. "I'm sorry we made you upset, but both the school and, more importantly, the hospital wanted you to stay home for a few days."

"But I'm *fine*," Kelcie felt the need to point out once again.

He shook his head at her. "I know you think that it's completely unnecessary, but we're not trying to protect everyone else from you, Kelcie. We're just trying to make sure our little girl is all right before sending her out where we can't get to her quickly if suddenly she's not. Does that make sense?"

Kelcie simply stared at him for a moment, then smiled. "Yeah, I guess so. I'm sorry, Dad. I was a real jerk-face earlier."

Mr. Pryce laughed. "Yes, you were that, but I understand. You need to learn to control your temper, but this is a brand new experience for all of us. It's completely understandable that we're all flustered about it. Just try to do better, all right?"

Kelcie nodded and smiled before hugging her father. "Okay. Thanks, Dad."

He gave her a squeeze. "I love you, little one. You know that?"

Kelcie nodded against his shoulder. "I love you, too, Daddy."

And she knew they both always would.

"Cliff, could you come help me set the table?" Mrs. Pryce's voice called from the kitchen.

Mr. Pryce kissed his daughter gently on the forehead. "Will you be joining us, Kelcie?"

Kelcie nodded emphatically. *"Definitely!"*

Her father left the room with a chuckle, but before Kelcie could follow him, little Jimmy wandered in. "Hi, Kelcie. You still come down here?"

Kelcie rolled her eyes and wrapped her arms around the little scamp in a great big hug. "Yes, yes, I do, little J-man."

Jimmy groaned. "Kelcie. . . ."

She laughed at him as he tried to wriggle out of her grasp, then let him go. "Sounds like supper's gonna be ready soon, Jimmy. Did you wash up?"

He looked up at her with his big, blue-green eyes. "You finally retoin to our home, and all you can say is 'Did you wash up?'"

Kelcie shook her head. "I never left our home, and it's 'return' and you know it, Jimmy."

Her little brother stuck his tongue out at her, then ran as fast as his spindly legs could carry him toward the bathroom.

Kelcie's eyes grew wide as he bumped into the console table bearing her mother's most prized and doubtless most expensive possession—a genuine Ming Dynasty vase that had been in her family for five generations and counting—and just kept on his merry little way. She gasped as the vase began to tip over, reflexively reaching toward it even though she was standing at the far side of the room.

And she caught it.

She stood beside the table, priceless vase in both hands, shaking. Surge number sixteen had just coursed through her entire being. In a split-second, a *whoosh* like a rushing wind, that blue glow shining all around her, she had sprinted across the fourteen-foot distance to the vase and caught it.

After a moment, she carefully replaced the Ming vase on the table before she could drop it and break it herself, then sank into a nearby chair. She leaned her elbows on her knees with her chin in her hands, willing herself to stop shaking, wondering how in the world she did that.

"What's happening to me?" she mumbled so quietly no one could have heard her even if anyone had been in the room with her.

When her mother called her in for supper about five minutes later, Kelcie had succeeded in composing herself outwardly. Inside, she was whimpering in confusion, but she was not about to let her family see that.

* * * *

The rest of the day and quite a bit of the next came and went without incident. No more surges occurred, although the faint warm and fuzzy feeling lingered on after the last one. Kelcie continued to wonder about it—and was determined to figure out how she had moved so fast.

After supper that night, Kelcie asked her parents, "Hey, can I head out for a while? I mean, I still feel all right, and it was really just a 'stay home from school' order, not a 'stay out of fresh air entirely' order, wasn't it?"

Her father crossed his arms and leaned back in his chair. "I suppose she really didn't say 'stay in the house, period,' did she? What do you think, hon?"

Mrs. Pryce bit her lip. "I don't know . . . I guess it's all right, if you think so, dear."

Mr. Pryce nodded. "Very well, you may 'head out' for a while, Kelcie. Don't make *too* late a night of it, though; nine thirty, ten at the latest. Do you hear me, Kelcie Olivia?"

Kelcie grinned. "Thanks, guys!"

She hugged and kissed her mother and father, then ruffled little Jimmy's hair on the way by as she made her escape to the great outdoors.

It was barely 6:45 when she jogged out to the 'Forgotten Realm'—what she, Lacey, and a couple of other childhood friends used to call the big, vacant, overgrown lot behind the abandoned pizza place on Goldwind Street. It was the most secluded area that Kelcie knew of within a few blocks of her house. Not many people even realized it was back there, with the timber closing in around the back of the pizza place and blocking the lot from view.

Kelcie and her friends had just stumbled upon it while goofing off in the 'Woodlands'—the timber—one day, several years ago, and added it to their wonderful world of fantastical fun. Kelcie, for her part, had never told another soul about the place, and many times she would wander there when she just wanted to get away from it all and think for a while. It was peaceful, quiet, and free of annoying little brothers.

This time, however, she had not gone there simply to think. She wanted to see if she could make herself do what she did the night before—minus the vase, of course. Had that just been a figment of her imagination, or could she really have run that fast? The only way she knew to prove what it was and what it was not was to try to do it again.

Kelcie stood at one corner of the Forgotten Realm and focused her gaze on the far corner, about fifty yards away. She took a deep breath, got into a track-and-field stance, and she was off . . . for two or three regular girl running steps before she tripped in a patch of moss and face-planted in the dirt.

She propped herself up on her elbows and rubbed her nose. The fall did not bloody it, but it still smarted. She pushed herself to her feet and dusted herself off, then looked over at the far corner again. She was bound and determined that she was going to run over to it, whether with that glow-speed or not . . . preferably without falling on her face again.

She backed into the corner again, assumed her track position, and pushed off . . . halfway across the lot, at regular speed, face-planting once again.

"Really?" Kelcie groaned, pushing herself up off the ground with a slight wince and making her way back to her corner.

She took a *deep* breath, letting it out as slowly and calmly as she could. "Third time's the charm, right?"

She focused her gaze directly on the goal corner of the Realm. This time she positioned herself like an action hero—like Lady Speed, her favorite hero—instead of a track-and-field athlete. One arm forward, one back, legs following suit, she took another small breath. . . .

And suddenly her fuzzy tingle intensified, that bright blue glow shone all around her, and within seconds she had far exceeded running to her goal, ending up almost in the very center of the Woodlands timber, half a mile away from the lot by the time she managed to stop running.

Kelcie panted, not from lack of breath, but from astonishment. She knew this entire timber very well—

she knew exactly where she was at—but how did she get all the way out here? She took her cell phone out of her coat pocket and glanced at the time.

"Wow, it's still the same exact minute as when I started—with twenty-two seconds to spare!" she exclaimed. "And I'm all the way *out here*! How did I *do* that?"

She slipped her phone back into her pocket and just stood there in the middle of the timber for a moment. Then, her mouth shaping itself into an ornery little grin, she resumed her Lady Speed pose and tried again. It worked!

With that intense tingle, bright glow, and odd, yet pleasant wind-passing-through-her sensation, she was running faster than she ever dreamed possible. When she was Jimmy's age—and, being honest, still somewhat now—she had always wondered what it would be like to *be* Lady Speed. Now she was living her wildest dreams. She had super-speed!

She zipped and zoomed out of the Woodlands and all over the town of Mapleborough, scaring about a dozen cats, at least two stray dogs, and one little old lady. The last one she felt kind of embarrassed about, knowing Mrs. Collier very well from her days at the elementary school nurse's station. She had been a rather rough-and-tumble child, and ended up there a lot as a grade-schooler.

When she finally stopped again, Kelcie found herself on the opposite side of town, about as far from her house as she could get without leaving the bounds of Mapleborough altogether. In fact, after a brief inspection of her surroundings, she realized that she was standing behind the pretty stone "You are now leaving

Mapleborough; we hope you come back soon!" sign on the outskirts of town.

"Whoa, if my parents knew I was all the way out here, they would ground me for a month—probably two!" Kelcie exclaimed, laughing. "This is *so* cool!"

She leaned against the stonework and pulled out her phone again. All that running, and it was only 7:35 . . . she could barely believe it.

"*Well*," she said, drawing out the word. "If I still have so much time before curfew . . . let's do it again!"

She assumed her action pose and took off like a stream of blue light.

The next thing she knew, she had halted in her friend Lacey's backyard. When she realized where she was at—and that the Dumonts were having a telescope night, taking turns looking at the moon, Mars, and such, more than likely—she ducked behind the nearest tree.

Renee Dumont, Lacey's older sister, looked in her direction.

Uh-oh, she must have heard some rustling! Kelcie thought as she pressed herself against the tree and bit her lip. After Renee turned away again, she let out the breath she'd been holding. Kelcie quietly made her way back to the gate and sped off, finishing her evening run back at the Forgotten Realm.

"Phew, that was close," Kelcie admonished herself, shaking her head. Then she tilted it. "And yet . . . I . . . want to tell Lacey about this."

She could not believe the words even as she spoke them. She had gone from wanting to hide her condition, to wanting to tell somebody.

No, not just *somebody*—her best friend.

She walked back to Lacey's house, a couple blocks from the Realm. She peeked into the Dumonts' yard, but they were gone. She slipped through the fence and behind the tree again and took out her phone. After making sure it was on silent, so she would not signal her presence in the backyard, she began to text Lacey.

Hey, Lace, are you busy?

No, I'm just sitting in my room, finishing my last two Geometry problems for the night. Before Kelcie could reply, Lacey added, *Oh, sorry, you probably didn't want to hear about me acing old geometry, Kelce-nemesis extraordinaire, did you? Oopsy.*

Ha-ha, very funny, Lacey.

What are you doing? Not just sitting at home bored, I hope.

No, not exactly, Kelcie responded. *Mom and Dad let me out of the house for a while; I still have about an hour or so 'til curfew.*

Oh, really? Awesome, Kelce!

So do you have a minute?

I guess. Why?

Because I'm right outside your house, Kelcie keyed. *And really want to talk to you *in person*, if that's all right.*

There was a pause before Lacey replied, *You're . . . what?*

In your backyard, on the side of the old oak nearest the fence. Can you come out here for a minute?

Then Kelcie added, *And please, don't tell your parents I'm out here. Just tell them you forgot something outside while you were telescoping, all right?*

Sure, but how do you know we were doing that?

I'll explain when you get out here. Come on, Lace; please?

All right, just give me a minute. Got one more theorem to write down, and I think I'm done with my homework, Lacey answered.

OK.

A few minutes later, Lacey emerged onto her back porch, looking around. Kelcie waved from behind the tree and waited for Lacey to make her way over.

"All right, I'm here, sneaking around in my own yard at eight-fifty-two at night," Lacey said, confused. "What's up, Kelce?

For a moment Kelcie could not get herself to do anything but grin.

"Kelcie, spit it out! I can't stay out here all night!" Lacey whispered hoarsely, glancing around the tree trunk at the back door for an impatient parent or sibling.

"I have super-speed," Kelcie finally managed to squeak out.

Lacey just stared at her for a moment. "What are you talking about? Did you hit your head or something?"

Kelcie laughed softly. "Well . . . yes, a couple times, but that's not the point, Lace! I have super-speed, like Lady Speed . . . only not exactly like hers. But still . . . I have *powers* now, Lacey!"

Lacey looked uncomfortable. "Kelcie, be serious, now. Like a hero is going to come from little old Mapleborough. That's just ridiculous."

"I'm dead serious, Lacey," Kelcie retorted, taken aback. "And I can prove it!"

She looked at the Dumonts' door, then shot off and back again, spreading her arms out once she had stopped. "See?"

Lacey had watched her friend very closely as she sped away, taking in the stream of blue glowing light as she left and returned. "Wow, I guess you do, don't you. . . ?"

"Thanks for sounding so enthused, Lace," Kelcie said, rolling her eyes. "This is exciting! I'm a living, breathing action hero!"

"You . . . you've done heroics? Saved the citizen and all that stuff?"

Kelcie paused. "Well, no. I *just* got my powers. I've been trying to figure them out all evening. I'm not going to just speed into the nearest gang war and try to stop it before really knowing what I can do, Lace. I'm not suicidal.

"I'm just . . . having the best time of my life! I could have had no hands, but instead, I got super-speed. This is *amazing*!"

Lacey's eyes widened. "*No hands*? You're gonna need to catch me up on that one."

Kelcie spent the next five minutes giving an overall summary of the situation, and Lacey just nodded slowly. "Yeah, we're going to have to talk more in depth to finish getting all of that straight."

She cleared her throat. "But, until then, I have a great idea."

"What's that?"

"You remember that costume I made you for Halloween a few months ago?"

Kelcie shook her head. "I am not going to be the hero in the princess secret agent costume, Lacey. That's from a movie."

"No, no, I know that, but I just mean that I still have all your measurements and a lot of materials, and you know that I'm a wizard with a sewing machine. I got that costume done in two afternoons—would have only needed one, except I broke three zippers before I finally found some that worked."

"Wait, are you saying what I think you're saying?"

Lacey grinned. "Come on."

Both girls went stealthily to the door. "Run up to my room like you ran just a little while ago when I open the door . . . all right?"

Kelcie grinned and nodded.

Lacey opened the door and up zipped Kelcie. Lacey closed the door fast.

"Wow, sure is windy out there!" She called in to her parents.

"Did you find what you were looking for, Lacey? You took an awful long time out there," her mother's sweet-toned voice answered.

"Yeah, just took a little longer than I thought it would. Sorry, Mom."

"It's all right. Did you finish your homework?"

Lacey bit her lip and crossed her fingers behind her back.

"Almost," she replied. Really, she *was* done, but she had to have some explanation for shutting herself back in her room.

"All right, hurry up. It's almost bed-time."

"Mom," Lacey dragged out the word.

"It's a school night."

"I know. . . ."

Lacey trudged up the steps to her room, finding Kelcie occupied with one of her pencils and a sheet of paper.

"And I didn't even have to ask you to sketch out your costume. Kids grow up so fast," she said in mock-sorrow after shutting the door and walking over to her best friend.

Kelcie laughed softly. "Real best friends are like twins; they can read each other's minds. Right?"

Lacey laughed in return, then peered at Kelcie's drawing.

Kelcie covered it up.

"I'm almost done, hold on," she reprimanded her. Once Lacey had obediently looked away, she resumed her drawing. "Do you have any good blues and silvers, Lace?"

Lacey nodded, still looking away. "I think so. Want me to go find some samples to show you?"

"That'd be great. I'm almost done."

"Well, then, I'll go get them while you're finishing up."

A few minutes later, around nine-thirty, Kelcie added the finishing touch to her costume design and spun the desk chair around to tell Lacey. Her eyes widened when she saw that Lacey's bed was half-covered by some of the prettiest shades of blue and silver fabric she had ever seen. "Wow, Lace . . . that's a lot to choose from."

Lacey grinned. "And this isn't even all of it. These *are* all of the materials I have best suited to running, though, I think. Come take a look."

The next twenty minutes were spent picking fabrics and shades and making re-measurements and slight design alterations to improve on Kelcie's general idea for the costume.

Lacey looked up at the clock. "Oh, Kelcie, it's 9:50! You need to head home, and I need to clean all this up before my parents come in to say good night."

Kelcie nodded and gave her best friend a big hug. "You think I can ask if I can come over tomorrow, *officially* this time?"

"You'd better try!" Lacey paused. "I'll ask my parents in the morning. They're leaving for an anniversary cruise before I get home from school, so it'll just be Renee, Jeff, and me at home. I hope you can come over."

"Me, too." Kelcie looked up at the clock. "Gotta run!"

She opened the bedroom window, climbed out onto the low awning, and slid herself over the edge, then dropped to the ground. She sped off toward home, arriving at exactly 9:58, two minutes before final curfew. She entered, bid her parents good night, and went up to her room. Throwing on her Lady Speed pajamas, she tried in vain all night long to get some sleep.

* * * *

Kelcie spent an extremely fidgety morning and afternoon the next day. She thought Lacey was never going to text her. She knew Lacey had school that day, but it was only supposed to be half a day. 12:30 rolled around.

Well, okay, she's probably grabbing some lunch and was told to finish her homework before inviting me over, Kelcie mused. *That's fine.*

3:00. *Does Lacey have a huge book report to do, or what? Surely she's done with her homework by now. Did her parents say no? She could still text me that, though. What's taking her so long?*

Finally, around 4:30, Kelcie's cell phone buzzed. She pounced on it like a hungry tiger, swiping the stupid 'Read Text' bar about seven times before it would actually swipe.

They said ok.

Kelcie just stared at the screen blankly for a moment, then furiously pounded the keys. *It took you until 4:30 to text me three little words?*

I've been busy with school and work, Kelce.

You had *that* much homework?

Not all just school-related, came Lacey's reply.

What do you mean?

Ask your mom and dad if you can come over after supper, say 6:30-ish. I'll show you when you get here.

Kelcie sighed at her phone. then typed, *All right, fine. Just give me a minute, and I'll get back to you with their answer.*

Kelcie stuffed her phone in her pocket and slid down the stairway banister.

"Kelcie! If we've told you once, we've told you a thousand times. Don't do that. You're going to hurt yourself," her father admonished her.

"Or inadvertently teach Jimmy to do it, and *he'll* hurt himself," her mother agreed.

"I'm sorry," Kelcie truthfully apologized. "I wasn't thinking; I just did it. Anyway, can I go over to Lacey's house after supper tonight?"

Mr. Pryce raised a brow. "I'm guessing you've already been in contact with Lacey about it?"

Kelcie grinned. "You know me so well. She said her parents said 'ok.' They won't be there tonight, but Lacey's big sister and brother will be, so we shouldn't be able to get into *too* much mischief."

Kelcie had to laugh.

Both of her parents smiled and shook their heads.

"Well, all right," her father conceded. "I suppose if it's all right with them, it's all right with us . . . this time."

"Just be back by ten at the latest since I need to get up for my appointment in the morning, right?"

Mrs. Pryce put her arm around her daughter. "That's my girl."

Kelcie grinned again and hugged her mom. "Hey, I know you guys, too, you know."

Mrs. Pryce gave her a squeeze in return. "When are you expected over there?"

"Six thirty-ish."

Her mother looked up at the clock on the mantle. "Well, then, I'd better whip up that casserole and stick it in the oven now, shouldn't I? You want to help me today, Kelcie?"

Kelcie nodded. "Sure! I just need to text Lacey that you said I could come over, and I'll be right there. Okay?"

* * * *

About 6:00, Kelcie told her parents good-bye and headed out the door. She smirked to herself as she shut it behind her. She definitely did not need half an hour to get to Lacey's, but that was fine with her.

She made sure no one was around, then ran off to the Forgotten Realm again and raced through the Woodlands for twenty minutes or so, sure that she had frightened every squirrel that had woken up from hibernation so far—and possibly scared more out of hibernation on her way past. Finally, she zipped over to Lacey's street and walked on the sidewalk like a normal person up to her house. She was still a couple of minutes early, but Lacey *had* said 6:30-*ish*.

Lacey looked almost flustered with her when she opened the front door. "*There* you are!"

"Whoa, it's still not quite the time appointed, Lace."

Lacey grinned. "I know, but I just have something I *really* want to show you, and I can hardly wait!"

Kelcie chuckled at her. "Well, let me in the door and take me to see it then, why don't ya?"

Lacey blinked. "Oh, right, duh! Come on, come on, come on!"

Kelcie barely had time to shout a "Hello!" to Renee and Jeff Dumont as Lacey practically dragged her up the stairs to her room.

"I can't believe *I'm* saying this right now, but *slow down*, Lace! What's the rush?" she inquired hoarsely.

Lacey grinned again. "Close your eyes."

"Lacey...."

"Come on, close 'em. It's a surprise!"

Kelcie rolled her eyes, then closed them as ordered. She shook her head as Lacey let out a quiet, excited, teenaged-girl squeal, then she heard the door unlatch and was pulled through it into the room. The door latched behind her, and Lacey pushed her over to the center of the room and turned her to the left.

"Can I open my eyes now?"

"Just *one* second...." Lacey's voice sounded muffled, as if she was speaking from under a blanket.

Kelcie blinked. "What...?"

"Close 'em!"

She squeezed her eyes shut.

What seemed like an eternity later—really only a minute or so at most—Lacey gave her a few rapid pats on the arm. "Okay, okay, okay ... look. Ta-da!"

Kelcie opened her eyes, then her mouth. It was gorgeous.

Before her, on one of her best friend's bright pink mannequins, was her costume design brought to life. A one-piece jumpsuit adorned the mannequin, a rich, cobalt blue with silver lightning bolts running from the wrists of the sleeves, over the shoulders, and crossing at the top of the chest to strike down both sides to the ankles of the legs. A thin outline of white bordered the lightning to make it really pop. At the base of the mannequin sat a pair of matching blue boots and gloves, lightning patterned perfectly in sync with the main costume. A matching blue mask, draped across the outstretched hand of the mannequin, completed the ensemble.

Kelcie finally let out one of Lacey's squeals.

"This is so awesome!" She stepped forward, reaching out and touching one of the sleeves. "What is this stuff? It almost looks leather-ish, but it feels like athletic wear, only thicker."

Lacey nodded. "It *is* athletic wear type stuff, mixed with a little Kevlar for extra protection and durability for the speed and such."

Kelcie slowly turned toward Lacey. "How did you get *Kevlar*?"

Lacey's eyes went huge. "Umm . . . well . . . I'll tell you later. Try it on! I want to see how it fits!"

A few minutes passed, and Kelcie stepped back out of Lacey's bathroom into the bedroom, all suited up. She felt like a little kid, a superstar, and a crazy person, all at the same time. She *loved* it!

"A-mazing! I can't believe you *made* this, Lace!"

"*You* can't believe it? *I* can barely believe it . . . it looks so cool!" Lacey countered, her expression almost like that of a proud mother as she beamed at her best friend, the super-speedster. "Does it fit ok?"

Kelcie stretched and made a few totally uncoordinated fighting motions to test out its mobility. "Well, I'll need to work on action skills if I'm going to pull this thing off, but I seem to be able to move around in it without too much pull—and no ripping sounds, so that's always good, too."

Lacey nodded emphatically. "*Extremely* so. Now we just need to come up with an equally amazing codename to go along with the suit, and—cosmetically speaking—we'll be well on our way to herodom."

Kelcie smirked. "Who's 'we,' Pale-face? I thought I was the one with powers."

She giggled and gave Lacey a friendly punch in the arm.

Lacey bit the inside of her cheek, then smiled in return. "Yeah, well, I know, I just meant . . . I *did* supply that suit, you know. I have a . . . whatchamacallit . . . *vested* interest in your heroism, too."

She shrugged, unable to keep from laughing at herself.

Kelcie shared the laugh with her. "Okay, that's true."

"So . . . any ideas?"

Kelcie paced the room a few times, rubbing her chin. "I don't know . . . something simple, not too flashy."

Lacey nodded. "Right . . . like Lady Speed!"

Kelcie put her hand on her friend's arm and shook her head. "That name's already taken, Lacey. We don't need to have *two* Lady Speeds out there confusing everybody."

She blushed a little behind the mask. "Unless you just meant simplicity-wise, then something like that, yeah."

Lacey laughed at her mixed-up friend. "Of course not *actually* Lady Speed, you dork. How about . . . Glow Speed?"

"No, that's my power. I don't want to be named *exactly* my power. How lame is that?"

Lacey nodded. "Right. So . . . Merenthia? Hey, that sounds cool. Because you got the speed after getting merenthium spilled on you?"

Kelcie rolled her eyes. "Yeah, exactly. People could put two and two together and come up with 'Kelcie Olivia Pryce' way too easily."

Lacey tilted her head a little sideways and nodded. "True. What about—"

"Speedette!"

Lacey blinked. "What did you just say?"

Kelcie giggled. "Speedette. It combines your wanting me to go by my power and my wanting to go simple. The only way I could go much simpler would be just plain Speed, or Fast, or Quick, or something lame like that. I think Speedette sounds cool. Lace?"

Lacey looked up at the ceiling with a thoughtful expression on her face, then back down at Kelcie with a grin. "Speedette! If it works for you, I think that's perfect!"

Kelcie nodded. "Then it's Speedette!"

The two shared another little squeal, hugging each other and bouncing up and down as two teen-aged best friends are wont to do. When they parted, Lacey whipped out her phone and snapped a quick picture, then sat down on the edge of her bed and woke up her laptop.

Kelcie gave her a confused smile. "What're you doing, Lace?"

Lacey stopped her hands over the keyboard. "Setting up a 'newest hero' page on CrazeBook, what else?"

Kelcie's eyes nearly bugged out of her head. "No, Lacey, stop! There's a reason that's called 'CrazeBook,' you know. It's *crazy* to put anything on there!"

Lacey looked at her strangely. "Why? People put dumber things than this up all the time. While 'newest hero' isn't a common one, I'm not the first to think it up, you know."

Kelcie's jaw dropped in exasperation. "Yeah, but how many of them do you think are *really* true? Most of them are probably just 'cool' kids trying to amp up their 'coolness.' They could be putting their whole families in danger when they aren't even really heroes!"

Kelcie shook her head decisively. "I'm not going to put Mom, Dad, and even Jimmy in danger like that. Don't do it, Lace; promise me!"

Lacey stared at her for a moment, mouth opening slightly, but no words coming out. She glanced down at her laptop again with an odd frown on her face, then her fingers flew like lightning over her keyboard before she slammed her laptop shut and tossed it to the other end of the bed.

Kelcie blinked at her strange friend. "What was that all about? Just decided to try and break your computer, or what?"

Lacey took a quick breath. "Ah, nothing, I just. . . ."

She grabbed the backpack sitting by her bed. "I need to do my homework, now. I'll . . . I'll see you later?"

Kelcie gave her a blank look, then nodded. "All . . . right, I guess."

"Oh, could you change again and leave the costume here? I did see one thing that I really ought to tweak before you get into any action or something."

Kelcie shook her head once again, unbelieving. "*Sure. . . .*"

She changed back to her regular clothes in Lacey's bathroom and put the costume on the foot of Lacey's bed as she was directed. "See you around, Lace."

Lacey offered one of her usual smiles. "Bye, Kelce!"

Kelcie let out a silent sigh, then headed down the stairs, called a "Good-bye!" in to Renee and Jeff, and zipped back home again.

* * * *

The following morning, Kelcie got up and ready to head back out to the hospital with her parents to get the test results. She remained quieter than usual all the way to the hospital, and smiled for the first time that day when she saw Dr. Penelope's gently smiling face as she came out of her office into the waiting room.

"I have the results right here," she said, sitting down beside Kelcie's mother and opening the folder she held so that both parents could see. "Everything seems to be a-okay, as the kids say."

Kelcie's eyes widened. How could that *possibly* be?

Dr. Penelope nodded to a comment from Mr. Pryce. "Yes, a few things seem to have been running a little fast"—and Kelcie thought, *a little*?—"But she had just gone through quite the ordeal. That's probably all it was. I would like to do a follow-up checkup now, just to make sure, but she should be good to go."

Kelcie's parents nodded in unison, and her father further agreed with an "All right."

Dr. Penelope smiled again, then motioned for Kelcie to follow her. "Well then, right this way."

As soon as the door to the room was shut, Kelcie turned to face Dr. Penelope.

"A little fast?" she could not stop herself from asking.

A twinkle came into Dr. Penelope's eyes. "Maybe more than a little . . . Speedette."

At first Kelcie was simply petrified, then she reddened with anger. "I told Lacey not to post that!"

"I didn't, Kelcie."

Kelcie blinked and turned to face her friend, brow furrowing as she saw Lacey step out of a strangely large cabinet in the corner of the room. "What are you doing here? And . . . why were you in a cabinet?"

She looked between the two. "What's going on?"

Lacey's expression was a bizarre mixture of serious, apprehensive, and excited as she answered. "What's going on is, you have powers now, too, Kelcie. And, umm. . . ."

"And we know where you can go to learn to use them," Dr. Penelope supplied.

Kelcie's face took on a rather odd expression of its own. "Wha . . . what? Where?"

Lacey looked at Dr. Penelope, then gestured Kelcie into the cabinet. "Right this way."

Kelcie still looked at her strangely, but she slowly stepped into the cabinet anyway—fearing that curiosity was about to kill the cat, but unable to keep from it. She stepped out onto a medium-sized landing, a stairwell opening up in the far right-hand corner. When Lacey gestured again, the trio headed down the stairs—all five or six flights of them. Kelcie lost track.

By the time they reached the last three or four steps, Kelcie descended more slowly, looking around at the scene before her in awestruck wonder.

The stairs ended in a balcony, and in front of the balcony was a *huge* room. Kelcie's eyes travelled from a couple of girls swimming in a huge aquarium in the very center of the room—*without scuba gear*—to a boy on her left who was climbing the completely smooth walls, then a girl swinging into view from a ledge somewhere above her.

More surprising to her than all of these, however, was the miniature jumbotron-type sign she found attached to the banister right in front of her.

"No *way* . . . this is *unreal*!" she exclaimed, turning to Lacey and pointing at the sign.

Lacey grinned at her. "No, no, this is *totally* real, Kelce."

Kelcie turned her dumbfounded, open-mouthed face to Dr. Penelope. "You're . . . you're *that* Penelope?"

Dr. Penelope laughed, then nodded at her with that gentle smile. "As the sign says, 'Welcome to the Young Champions.'"

SCIONS OF STARMOOR: THE GIFTING OF PENELOPE PETTIGREW

BY

C.K. DEATHERAGE

Penny breathed deeply, heavily, tossing her blonde head in her sleep. She wanted to be free. She could taste freedom in the air about her, could hear it on the currents that moved the clouds across the horizon, could feel it in the breeze that blew through the window. The yearning to be *out there*, one with the sky and the stars, was almost painful. Her throat tightened and tears rolled down her cheeks wetting the soft fabric of the pillow beneath her. A sob caught in her throat–and she awoke with a start and a gasp, sitting up quickly and wiping her face with the back of her hand.

She took in several deep breaths to calm herself. What was going on? Every night for the past two weeks she had experienced the same wretched dream.

Reaching over to the rickety nightstand beside her, she pulled out a tissue and blew her nose, hoping the Twins across the hall didn't hear. They had a strange obsession with seeing her cry—they loved it, especially if they were the cause of her tears. She sighed and leaned back against her pillow, gazing out the small window of her bedroom at the stars glittering against the black of the night sky.

She wondered at her dream. The emotions were so strong, so visceral. Did she really feel that way about her home?

Her lips twitched into a wry smile. *Home.* This house had not been her home since her father died. Her birth mother had died when she was two. She could only remember a few images of a dark-haired woman with enchanting brown eyes and the tune to a wordless song that her mother used to sing to her.

But five years ago, for some reason, Dad had decided she needed a new mother and had met Genevieve Rachel Dupont at work. A year later, they were married, and Genevieve and her twin daughters, now age sixteen, had moved in.

Again, Penny felt a soft sigh escape her lips. She shook her head, still gazing at the stars. The first two years had been fun, and it seemed like they could be a true family together. Then her father developed cancer. He lingered for a year, painfully, his body wasting away.

She didn't know if it were her father's suffering that changed Genevieve, or if her step-mother's true nature just had the freedom to express itself after her father died, but Genevieve became a monster, and her two daughters, Scarlett and Chartreuse, were monsterettes. They turned her into a veritable Cinderella, foisting off most of the household duties onto her, even while she worked at Berticelli's Pasta House part-time to earn enough money to supplement the fast dwindling life insurance her father had left them.

She gritted her teeth until they hurt. She had just turned eighteen, which meant she could legally leave home. And she planned to—oh yes, she planned to . . . that is, once she finished her senior year. Let the Twins do their own laundry for a change! Maybe that was why she kept having the dreams. Still, it was disturbing to have such strong feelings invade her sleep cycle.

She wiped a lock of blonde hair from her eyes as she forced herself to relax and try to resume sleep. Suddenly, a feeling of panic engulfed her, a sense of imminent danger. Her heart began to pound.

She sat up and peered around her small room, sensing an intruder nearby. But no one was there. No one. Yet the feeling persisted.

She stood up quietly, pulling on her robe, and moved towards the door. Before opening it, she listened carefully. Then her eyes widened. The intruder was downstairs. Their new parakeet was making an awful whistling and clacking racket from the living room where its cage sat next to the large double window.

Penny glanced around her room, looking for something she could use as a weapon and spied her knitting basket. She jerked out an unused pair of long needles, opened the door quietly, and stepped into the hall. Why Genevieve and the Twins weren't panicking with the noise from the frantic bird, she couldn't understand.

In fact, she could hear snoring from the Twins' room and music playing softly from her step-mother's bedroom. Of course, they'd leave it up to her to investigate. Again, she gritted her teeth, swallowing her anger and frustration.

Stepping carefully down the stairway, one knitting needle clutched in either hand, Penny rounded the corner of the hallway and edged past the living room door, casting her eyes in all directions. The light of the moon shining through the large window lit up the room fully, and Penny stood, puzzled. The bird still whistled and chirped wildly, but there was no one there.

Then she saw it—or, rather, *him*. Beelzebub, the sleek orange tabby that Scarlett and Chartreuse insisted they adopt from a kid who was giving away kittens at Smitty's Grocers parking lot. They only wanted it because she had wanted the tiny calico that was obviously the runt of the litter. But the Twins had gotten their way, bringing home the feisty tabby whom they named Barnabas. Penny secretly called him *Beelzebub* for his rather demonic demeanor.

That was eight months ago, and the feline had grown into a large, sleek attack machine. Beelzebub had it in for her, lying in wait and pouncing when she least expected it, tearing holes in her nylons, and occasionally defecating in her closet. Now he was after Chirps, the parakeet.

The cat crouched beneath the cage, green eyes glittering with hunting-lust, as he suddenly launched his sleek form into the air and grappled with the bird cage, causing it to swing madly. Chirps battered herself against the wires in desperation.

"Aah!" Penny felt her legs go weak as she stumbled back, leaning against the wall, heart beating as frantically as Chirps' wings. She felt the knitting needles drop from her tingling hands and heard them clatter on the hardwood floor. What was wrong with her? She felt terrified . . . terrified of Beelzebub, of all things.

As if sensing her fear, the cat dropped from the swinging cage and turned to face her, pacing slowly in her direction, voicing a rolling growl, hair on end.

Penny's breath came in sharp gasps as she tried to back up, but found the wall blocking her way. She locked eyes with the menacing feline, and suddenly, a new set of emotions washed over her. Her muscles tensed, and she felt the hair at the nape of her neck rise—not with fear but with a feral sense of the hunt. She felt strong, intimidating, powerful. She was aware of every inch of her body, which muscles were flexed, which relaxed. She knew just how far she would need to leap to . . . to do what?

She took a step toward Beelzebub, who stopped in his tracks and arched his back.

"Barnabas," she said in a low, threatening tone, using the cat's given name. "You may *not* eat Chirps, and you may *not* pounce on me. Now go back to your kitty bed and wait for your canned cat food in the morning."

With a deep-throated *huff*, the yellow tom turned and sauntered over to the corner where his burgundy cat cushion sat on the floor next to the couch. He stood there, massaging the pillow a few moments with his front paws before deciding to plop down with another *huff*, softer this time. But he kept his eyes firmly on Penny.

Penny blinked. The cat had actually obeyed her. Usually, she felt lucky if he just ignored her rather than reach out and swipe at her with his front paw.

"Okay, then. Good, Kitty," she said, walking slowly towards Chirps' cage. "Now, stay put."

Beelzebub sighed and rested his large head on his front paws, though his tail occasionally twitched.

Penny felt his gaze on her as she neared the bird's wire home. Strangely, that sense of power and visceral strength began to fade and her heart began to flutter fearfully the closer she got to Chirps. She took a deep breath to calm herself, and as she did so, she noticed the parakeet stop beating herself against the bars of the cage and settle on her perch.

She reached through the wires and stroked the small creature with her finger. "There now, ol' Beelzebub is not going to eat you for dinner. He's well-fed as is."

The Twins had purchased Chirps just two weeks ago, though—Penny frowned thinking back on the event—*she*, of course, had the duty of feeding and watering the small bird and cleaning out its cage twice a week. She shook her head. She loved animals–well, *most* animals. Beelzebub was a notable exception, but she did feel the Twins ought to do their fair share of pet up-keep. Wishful thinking.

A light breeze blew in through the screened-in window, tickling along her cheeks and blowing a few strands of her hair. Chirps whistled sadly, and suddenly, Penny felt that incredible longing to be free, to float above the city, to fly with the stars that she had felt in her dreams. Chirps sat there, small eyes cocked at her, and Penny felt her heart speed up.

"No," she whispered, stepping away from the cage. "No, this isn't possible!"

She looked away from the bird and fixed her gaze on the cat. At once, the painful yearning left her, and she felt relaxed, content, with a strange but not unpleasant tickle in her throat. Beelzebub was drifting in and out of sleep, purring softly to himself.

"No!" she gasped, turned, and ran from the room, up the stairs, and into her bedroom, closing the door behind her as quietly as she could. She leaned against it, heart beating rapidly, her hands sweating.

"I'm going crazy." Tears sprang to her eyes. "I'm nutso!"

She tried to breathe in slowly, tried to think clearly, tried anything to keep from conjuring the insane thought she'd had downstairs. Nothing was working.

I can feel them. She drew a shuddering breath as at last the thought manifested itself. *I can hear their thoughts—and they can hear mine.*

Shakily, she moved toward her bed and climbed in, pulling the covers up to her chin. She sighed, closing her eyes. A single tear slipped through. As if her home life wasn't bad enough, now she was undoubtedly suffering from a nervous breakdown.

She drew in a deep breath and exhaled slowly. Maybe a good night's sleep would give her a better perspective. She just prayed it would be dreamless.

* * * *

The alarm startled her as its shrill repetitive beep jarred Penny from an exhausted sleep. She groaned as she rolled over to shut it off. Time to fix breakfast for Genevieve and the Twins—and, of course, feed Beelzebub. She sat up, letting the covers slide down her torso, and stretched.

Then she remembered. *Beelzebub . . . Chirps. . . .*

She swallowed. Had it all been a dream? A rather frightening, fantastic dream? She stood up, reaching for her clothes draped over the foot of her bed. She shook her head as she dressed. Surely, she had dreamed the event from last night. She certainly felt nothing weird now—except tired. But that was normal.

With a sigh, she stumbled to her door and held on to the banister as she slowly paced down the steps. She tried to avoid the squeaky parts so as not to awaken the others too soon. She was too tired to deal with their early-morning crankiness—at least before she had a cup of coffee.

At the bottom of the stairs, the cat came bounding up to her, rubbing its yellow-orange body against her leg.

"Barnabas?" she whispered, confused. He was definitely acting strange. Normally, he snubbed her while leading the way to the kitchen for her to open a can of cat food and plop it on a plate for him. Never had he actually shown a sign of affection for her, despite her duties of feeding him and scooping his boxes.

She shook her head and tried to walk around the feline, pausing in the doorway of the living room to check on Chirps—just in case the cat's happy mood came from an unexpected feathery dinner. But the parakeet sat quietly on her perch next to the window, cocking her head at her and uttering a few "feed me" trills.

She smiled. "I'll get to you. Let me take care of you-know-who first."

She turned to head toward the kitchen but stumbled with an exclamation of pain as something sharp poked into her toe. Looking down, she spied two knitting needles lying on the floor next to the doorway. Her eyes widened as she bent down to rub her toe and pick up the offending instruments. She stared at them in her hands and her throat grew tight.

"It really happened!" she whispered, heart beginning to thump erratically. "It wasn't a dream!"

"*Meowr.*"

Penny suddenly felt quite hungry, her stomach growling impatiently. She looked at Beelzebub and swallowed. The cat sat there, gazing at her with large yellow eyes, tail twitching.

She licked her lips. "Are you hungry, Beel—ah—Barnabas?"

She tried to keep her voice steady. The cat meowed again and again commenced to rubbing its body against her legs. She decided to try something—something entirely crazy.

She closed her eyes and *thought* at the cat. *Go to the kitchen and wait for me by your dish.*

Opening her eyes, she spied Beelzebub's orange tail as he trotted around the corner towards the kitchen. She swallowed and followed slowly. Sure enough, when she entered the room, there sat her nemesis quietly by his food dish, looking expectantly at her.

With shaking hands, she set down the knitting needles and opened a can of mushed cat food, crouching down to splat it on his plate. As the cat bent over to nibble on the pile, she reached out and tentatively stroked his fur. He began to purr and arch his back even as he continued to gobble his food.

Penny stood up, rubbing her forehead.

"Hoo, boy! This is entirely weird!" she muttered, then she turned and walked back to the living room.

Upon entering it, at once Chirps gave a happy whistle and began sharpening her beak on the cage.

Taking a deep breath, Penny opened the cage door and stepped back. She held out her hand, fingers straight and thought, *Fly to me.*

Immediately, she heard the flutter of wings, and the small blue and white parakeet alighted on her finger, cocking its head at her and blinking. The thought came into her mind that formed itself into a word—*food.* She swallowed, and with her free hand, she picked up the small container of birdseed and shook out a tiny mound onto the bird dish.

Return, she thought, and Chirps flew back to her cage, alighting on the side of the dish and began pecking at the small seeds.

Slowly, Penny shut the cage door. She walked over to a cushioned chair and plopped down, legs feeling a little shaky.

What is happening to me? She wondered.

"What's this?"

Penny glanced up to see her step-mother, clothed in pink Asian-style silk pajamas and robe, standing in the doorway.

"I—" Penny began, but Genevieve cut her off.

"The wonderful aroma of percolating coffee and crisping toast seems strangely absent this morning. You know we keep to a prompt and regular schedule in this house—and you are now fifteen minutes behind. Attend to your duties and quit daydreaming, Penelope."

"But—" Penny began, then thought better of it. Genevieve might just have her committed to the mental hospital if she told her what was going on. Or perhaps not. That would cost money, and Genevieve was not about to waste any of that on *her.* She sighed and stood to her feet. "Yes, ma'am."

It seemed her step-mom and the Twins dawdled eating breakfast, despite their "schedule," and by the time Penny had finished washing the dishes, she had missed the bus. That meant a long mile hike to the high school and probably time in detention for being late.

She sighed as she trotted up the sidewalk, head bent against a brisk Spring breeze. She paused as she neared the Tillerman's house. Behind a rather rickety chain-linked fence stood the Tillerman's Mastiff, Slasher, waiting for her to pass by. She was terrified of the beast. He would fling his massive body against the creaking gate, snarling and slinging great slobs of saliva all over the place as she would scurry by.

Today, however, was different.

As Penny approached the Tillerman's house, Slasher stood to his feet, ready to perform his menacing act.

Penny swallowed and aimed a thought at the dog. *Sit still and be quiet.*

Slowly, the massive furry hulk sat down on its haunches. It panted through large jaws, drool slipping down and wetting its ruff.

Good boy, she thought as she walked past. She heard a loud *thunking* noise and glanced back to see Slasher waving its heavy tail, thumping it on the ground, as his jaws seemed to smile at her.

As her feet took her on beyond the house, Penny grinned to herself. She might be going crazy, but there was a lot of potential in this madness! School was a circus of experimenting with her new powers. In lab, she had the rats holding on to each other's tails and running circles in their cages, much to the consternation of the instructor. On break outside, she watched as the local robins bobbed and dipped in a gleeful ariel dance for her amusement. At lunch, she summoned the hidden mice from the kitchen to run pell mell through the cafeteria accompanied by the screams and shouts of startled students.

And after school, at Berticelli's Pasta House, as she bussed tables and washed dishes, she amazed herself by ordering the roaches that inhabited the space between the counters and the walls to march outside and disperse into the grassy field across the street. Franco Berticelli had tried for years to rid his restaurant of the pests, especially before certification inspections, but they always came back. She could not guarantee a new batch would not appear, but the former six-legged residents had had impressed upon them that the field was a better place to feed and reproduce—the only instincts their limited thinking capacity would let her manipulate.

Walking home that evening, passing the Tillerman's house on purpose and patting the tail-thumping Slasher over the fence, Penny came to a sobering conclusion. While she had had fun with her new-found abilities, what was the point of it all? Surely there had to be a reason for her sudden gift—besides the temptation to order a few of Berticelli's former residents to invade the Twins' room. A temptation she reluctantly set aside.

She chewed on her lower lip as she climbed the steps of the front porch and opened the door. What was she supposed to do with these powers? Become the world's best veterinarian? The greatest animal whisperer? An animal trainer like her Grandma May?

She shook her head as she hung up her jacket in the hall closet. There must be *something* she should be doing.

Beelzebub—*Barnabas*, she corrected—came bounding up to greet her, rubbing his body against her legs. She bent down to stroke him. Chartreuse, who had stepped into the hallway from the living room, frowned, her green eyes showing disapproval.

"Leave Barnabas alone," she snapped, placing one hand on her hip and flipping back her long brown hair. "Did you bring home dinner from Berticelli's?"

Penny swallowed, heart sinking. She'd been so wrapped up in her thoughts about her abilities, she'd forgotten about dinner. "No, I'm sorry. I forgot."

"Forgot!" Chartreuse rolled her eyes and turned towards the living room, yelling, "Mom, Penny forgot dinner—again!"

"No! Wait! I'll go back and get something." Penny could hear the desperation in her voice. She knew she'd be grounded for a week if she didn't remedy the situation.

"Too late, dear." Genevieve floated into the hall, her long auburn hair, piled elegantly on her head, while her tight-fitting shiny black pants emphasized her still-shapely hips. It was obvious she had a date. "You'll just have to fix something here at home for the girls, then take yourself to your room. You're grounded, of course."

Penny could feel herself growing angry. It was all so unfair! Why was *she* the only one who cooked or cleaned or did much of anything in the house? Why couldn't the Twins fix their own dinner?

She felt a movement by her feet and saw Barnabas dart towards Genevieve, hackles raised, a high-pitched growl emanating from his throat. *Oh no!*

Before she could utter or think of a command to stop, he had launched himself at her step-mother's face, claws sinking into the primped and painted cheeks. With a terrible shriek, Genevieve grabbed the cat and hurled him against the wall.

Penny gasped and collapsed to her hands and knees as pain exploded in her head. Then it receded into . . . nothing. She looked up, hearing her step-mother screaming as she rushed down the hall to the bathroom to check the damage done to her face.

Chartreuse followed her, adding her own sympathetic wails to the cacophony. Scarlett peeked her red-haired head out from the living room, took in the commotion in one quick glance and quickly retreated back to the living room, apparently judging it was safest to stay out of the way.

Penny breathed hard, tears coming to her eyes. She spied the cat's limp form lying against the wall and slowly stood and staggered to his body. She knew without touching him that he was dead. She had felt his life snuff out. Still she reached down and stroked his fur.

"I'm sorry," she whispered, then picking him up, she cradled his body in her arms. "I'm so, so sorry."

She knew somehow her anger had fueled his attack. Maybe her powers weren't a gift. Maybe they were a curse. She bent her head and wept, burying her face in Barnabas' fur.

While her step-mom continued to tend to her face, bewailing the damage, Penny carried Barnabas outside and laid him down beneath the red maple. She trudged to the shed and dug out the shovel.

Straining, she stamped down and hoisted out shovelful after shovelful of moist earth until she felt the hole was deep enough. Then, with a last loving embrace, she placed Barnabas' limp form in the hole and covered him up.

After putting the shovel back, she stood in the yard, trembling, thinking. She couldn't stay here. She had to find help, lest she bring more harm to others—both human and animal. But where could she go?

Vaguely, a thought began to form in her mind. She would leave and visit her grandmother, on her birth mother's side, in California. She hadn't seen Grandma May since her father had died. Even though her grandmother had offered to fly her out for visits, Genevieve had always found excuses to forbid it. Grandma May was the owner of "May's Critters," an animal training center, whose creatures often appeared in Hollywood movies.

Despite her fears and feelings, Penny found herself smiling. She remembered petting a lion and a bear as well as various dogs, cats, pigs, Toucans, parrots, and horses when she had last visited. If anyone could help her understand her newfound powers, Grandma May could.

She took a deep breath and trotted back into the house, ignoring Genevieve's distant cries of pain as she climbed the stairs to her bedroom to pull out from her desk drawer the stack of letters and cards her grandmother had sent over the years. She carefully tore out the corner from one, containing Grandma May's address and placed it in her wallet. Then she gathered and packed a few clothes in her travel bag, throwing in her favorite book, her brush, and a few other toiletries.

Finally, she walked to her trash can and carefully lifted it up. Taped to the bottom was an envelope containing about $1300—an amount scraped together a tiny bit at a time from her paycheck without Genevieve's knowledge. Gathering everything, she descended the stairs, softly, hoping to avoid detection. No such luck.

"You!"

She flinched as Genevieve's high-pitched screech cut the air.

"Where do you think you're going? And where's that wretched cat? Do you see what it did to me?"

Penny glanced up at her step-mom's face. Four long scratches on either cheek, still oozing blood, marred Genevieve's admittedly beautiful features.

She licked her lips, brushing back a strand of blonde hair from her face. "I'm sorry. And as for Barnabas, he's dead. I buried him."

"Good riddance! Whatever could have come over the beast?" Genevieve, paused, dabbing at her cheeks with a blood-stained washcloth. "I can't possibly go out looking like this, not with Daniel Stevetston! I'll have to call and cancel our date. Tell him I'm sick or something."

She glared at Penny. "Well, fetch me the phone! He could be here any time now."

Penny drew a deep breath. "You'll have to fetch it yourself. I'm leaving."

"Leaving! My dear girl, you'll do no such thing." Genevieve hesitated as she took in the travel bag slung over Penny's shoulder. Her green eyes snapped fire. "After all I've done for you, you're just going to walk out on your sisters and me? You ungrateful. . . ."

"Yes," Penny interjected before her step-mother could finish her tirade. "I'm afraid you'll have to learn to do without me and my cooking, cleaning, laundering, working, and otherwise maintaining the household. But first, I have to do one last thing."

Striding into the living room, Penny opened the cage and called Chirps to her finger. Carrying the bird to the front door, she opened it and let the bird fly free. She didn't know if the parakeet could adjust to life in the wild, but she knew the little bird yearned to try. She felt its exultant spirit as she saw it take wing to the sky.

She smiled and hoisted her bag higher on her shoulder and stepped down from the porch.

"You take one more step, young woman, and I'll call the police to hunt you down as a runaway!"

Penny shook her head and lowered her foot to the next step. "I'm eighteen, Genevieve. I can leave if I want to."

"You're not done with high school!"

Another step down. "I'll finish somewhere else."

"If you leave, you're on your own," Genevieve's voice cut like a frozen sliver on the air. "And don't come crawling back here—ever!"

With a small smile, Penny stepped down, placing her feet on the firm concrete of the walkway. Shifting her travel bag one last time, she lifted her chin, drinking in the Spring breeze that stroked her cheeks and ran its fingers through her hair.

She was free. Like Chirps. Like the sparrows that twittered, zig-zagging happily overhead as they shared her feelings. Her smile broadened.

Turning, she strode down the sidewalk, never once looking back.

Scions of Starmoor: Looking Back

By

C.K. Deatherage

Susan stopped at the red light, taking the opportunity to check her make-up in the mirror on the back of the sunshade. She pursed her lips and waggled her brows, thinking that her eye shadow made her look at least a little older than her eighteen years, though—she frowned—her long auburn hair, curly and a bit unruly, undermined the attempt to appear twenty-four.

At a honk, she sighed, tossed up the sunshade, and pressed on the gas pedal. She hoped the job interview she was heading for would pan out. A summertime position of daycare attendant, though not much more than a glorified babysitter, sounded so much better than a burger tosser or taco maker. She had boasted to her friends that her first job would be a step in her ultimate goal of corporate executive.

Her aunt was CEO of Dante's Hellfighters, a company of firefighters that had put out some of the world's worst oil rig conflagrations. As her aunt had remained unmarried and without children, that made Susan a likely candidate for her replacement—provided she proved herself in college and career.

Susan halted at a four-way stop, glancing both ways before stepping on the gas. She had made it halfway across the intersection when the sound of squealing tires caused her to jerk her head to the right. Her heart suddenly skipped and began pounding in her chest as she saw a bright red pickup swerving erratically, trying to avoid a collision.

Where did he *come from?*

She stomped on the accelerator, trying to move out of the way. Unfortunately, the driver of the pickup had the same idea, twisting his car to the right. Susan closed her eyes just as the red blur plowed into the passenger side of her Volkswagon. She felt her car slam and shudder as the pickup continued crunching its way into her small blue beetle.

Time seemed to slow as she watched the dented chrome bumper edge its way nearer to her driver's seat. She would be crushed. No job as a daycare attendant, no position in her aunt's corporation, no office as an executive. No dreams, no hope, no life.

She opened her mouth to scream. Her body jerked. Then her vision broke into a million colored shards, like crystal shattering, spreading its glistening fragments to the wind. . . .

She blinked then slammed on her brakes, coming to a stop just before crossing the four-way intersection. A large red pickup honked as it ran through its stop sign on the right and roared past her small blue beetle. Her hands shook on the steering wheel, and her breath came in sharp quick gasps. After looking carefully both ways, she slowly drove her car through the intersection, pulling off to the side as she waited for her trembling to stop. It took a while.

What had just happened? She rubbed her forehead. Had she hallucinated? Had she fallen asleep and dreamed the entire incident? But how could that explain the red pickup barreling past her in real life? No matter how she tried to understand the event, she ended up with the same answer.

Impossible!

Taking a deep breath, then exhaling slowly, she fought to calm her nerves. Glancing at the dashboard clock, she gasped. She would have to hurry to make her interview on time. No matter what the shock to her system or what delusion she had just experienced, she wouldn't let her fledgling career end without even starting.

Pulling into the parking lot of Pritchard's Childcare and Preschool, she hurriedly pushed her car door open, barely missing the vehicle next to her, and dashed through the entrance to the daycare.

"I'm here to see Miss Pritchard, please," she gasped out at the blonde-haired woman behind the Welcome Counter. She glanced at the clock on the wall and tried to relax. 1:02. She was two minutes late.

"Follow me, please."

Susan fell into step behind the blonde and walked past several rooms filled with laughter, sometimes crying, and always noisy small children.

"Miss Pritchard? Your interview is here," the blonde stood in the door of a small office and motioned toward Susan.

Susan stepped forward smiling.

An older woman, brunette with gray at her temples, looked up, her sharp brown eyes quickly assessing. "You're rather young, aren't you?"

So much for the maturing effects of eye-shadow.

"I'm eighteen, Ma'am."

Keep smiling.

"Hmm. You look more like sixteen to me."

"I have my driver's license with me if you need to confirm my age." Susan opened her purse to retrieve her wallet.

"That won't be necessary." Miss Pritchard leaned back in her chair. "I don't suppose you have a resume or portfolio?"

Susan licked her lips. Fortunately, her aunt had drilled into her the importance of careful record-keeping. She set down a manila folder. "Here's my portfolio, Miss Pritchard."

The older woman picked up the folder, opening it, and perusing the typed resume inside.

Susan waited, patient and smiling outwardly, but impatient inside. She was proud of her school record, her academic achievements, her community service.

"Not much experience working with children, I see."

Susan swallowed, then said, "I have a younger brother I used to babysit."

Miss Pritchard snorted. "And did you watch over your brother because you wanted to or because your parents insisted you do so?"

"Ah, sometimes one, sometimes the other?" Susan wasn't sure what her hopefully future employer wanted.

"Hmm." Miss Pritchard slowly closed the folder and handed it back. "We run a quality childcare center, Miss Roberts. Many of our clients are among the influential citizens of our community. They expect their children to be well-cared for by qualified persons. Not big sisters who may or may not have appreciated the chore of watching their younger brothers. Thank you for your time. You may go."

Susan blinked. The interview was over? Just like that? The fact that Pritchard's Child Care and Preschool catered to the well-to-do and VIPs was exactly *why* Susan wanted to work here. She could make connections that might be useful later in her career.

"I—but. . . ."

The woman waved her hand in dismissal, while looking down at a ledger she held in front of her. "I said you may go, Mis Roberts."

Susan backed out and closed the door. She took a few steps down the hall, then leaned against the wall, tears coming to her eyes.

Stupid! She gritted her teeth. *Stupid, stupid, stupid! She asked for childcare experience, and you tell her you babysat your brother? Stupid!*

She could have told the woman about volunteering in the church nursery once a month or helping at Camp Wantamelee as a game and sports helper last summer, albeit with gradeschool kids. Why hadn't she put *those* things in her portfolio?

She sighed, wiping her cheeks with the back of her hand before preparing to leave. Suddenly, she caught her breath, her head spinning dizzily.

"Unh...." she groaned, placing her fingertips against her temples, and leaned forward. As if through a hollow tunnel, she heard footsteps approaching.

"Ma'am are you alri—"

She felt herself falling. Then her vision exploded into colored fragments. . . .

"May I help you?"

Susan blinked. She was standing in front of the Welcome Desk, the blonde attendant smiling at her. Behind the woman, the wall clock read exactly 1:02 pm, the time she had stepped through the door for her interview. She felt a tremor pass through her body. It was happening again. Had she already been here? Had she experienced a vision of the future? What was going on?

"I—my name is Susan Roberts. I'm here to see Miss Pritchard." Her voice shook, and she tried to cover it with a smile.

The blonde woman nodded. "Follow me, please."

Again, they walked down halls past rooms of playing, sleeping, happy, or weeping toddlers. Again, they stood outside Miss Pritchard's office as the attendant introduced her. As if repeating a memorized performance, Susan saw herself handing the brown-haired woman her portfolio and bracing for the woman's dismissal.

"Not much experience with children, I see."

"Actually, I failed to mention in my resume that I volunteer once a month in the nursery at our church, and last summer I worked as an assistant to the sports coordinator for Camp Wantamelee. I can get you references, if you'd like."

Miss Pritchard closed the manila folder and handed it back. "You should have had your references included already. However, you seem well-educated and well-rounded. Come back tomorrow with your references, and I'll consider your application."

"I—yes, Miss Pritchard. And thank you." Holding her portfolio, Susan exited the office and strode confidently down the hall.

She could contact the Nursery Director at church and the Camp Coordinator tonight and have them email letters of reference. Surely, if the formidable Miss Pritchard was willing to give her portfolio a second glance, her chances of being hired were quite good!

Upon reaching her car, Susan paused, hand on the handle. She felt an odd churning sensation in her stomach as the two *deja vue* episodes replayed in her mind.

No, not deja vue, she mentally corrected. *That's a feeling of the same thing being repeated. These incidents differed.*

She took a deep breath, clearing her mind of the disturbing images. Opening the door and sliding into the seat, Susan started the car and backed out. She had too much to do to freak out over some weird mind trick her thoughts had played on her. There had to be a reasonable explanation, but for now that explanation—whatever it was—would have to wait.

Pulling her blue beetle into the parking lot of West Chesterton Credit Union, Susan hopped out of her car and strode briskly through the glass doors, while digging in her purse for her checkbook. She needed to transfer about $250 from savings to checking for next month's car payment.

Gradually, Susan felt a sense of unease. She looked up, realizing the credit union was unusually quiet. Then she swallowed, her open purse nearly slipping from her grip. Everyone—about seven people in all—was gathered in a corner near the clerks' counter. A man wearing a clown mask was staring in her direction, pointing a pistol at her.

"Welcome to our party," he smirked behind the latex. He flicked his gun towards the cowering customers. "Come join us."

She hesitated. The door was just a few feet away. Should she make a dash for it?

The clown seemed to read her thoughts. "I said join us . . . or would you rather I pull this trigger?"

Swallowing again, she nodded, snapping her purse shut and stumbling quickly over to the small crowd. She felt herself shaking as she took her place between a rather hefty man, whose face glistened with frightened sweat, and a twenty-something mother with a small girl, who clutched her child to her with a fierce protectiveness.

The clown glanced back at the clerk, even as he leveled his pistol at the customers. "Hurry up with that money. My finger has a nasty habit of twitching when I hear sirens."

Sirens. Susan's eyes widened as in the distance, she could discern sirens slowly drawing closer. A lot of them. Her eyes flicked back to the gun and the agitated man holding it.

Suddenly, she felt the woman next to her stiffen and cry out, "Ginny!"

Susan watched as though in slow motion as the small girl darted out of her mother's grasp and ran for the door. The mother started after her. Susan breathed hard as the clown whirled about and fired. The woman dropped to the floor, and her young daughter stopped, standing wide-eyed.

"No!" Susan gasped. She shifted to face the robber, the sirens sounding much closer now.

The man had the gun aimed back at the huddled group.

"Looks like we have to do this the hard way," he snarled, and his finger tightened.

Several things happened simultaneously. Echoing as if from a deep cave, Susan heard the gun fire again and saw the big man next to her stagger, even as she felt a sharp burning sensation penetrate her left side. Then her vision shattered into a thousand fragments. . . .

Susan drew a deep breath, blinking. The big man to her left continued to stand and sweat while the mother on her right murmured quietly to her daughter.

Her brow furrowed, confused, then she heard the clown growl out, "Hurry up with that money. My finger has a nasty habit of twitching when I hear sirens."

The young girl beside her moved.

Immediately, Susan whirled and flung an arm out just as the child tried to dart forward, giving the mother time to grasp her daughter's shoulders and pull her back.

"Thank you," the woman whispered, even as she clutched her daughter close.

Susan nodded, but her attention was elsewhere. Sirens. Distant. Faint, but coming closer.

For a moment, the clown looked away, head cocked, as if straining to hear from beneath his latex mask. Then he shook his head, returned his gaze to the corner, and aimed his handgun at the terrified customers. "Looks like we'll have to do this the hard way."

His finger tightened, and once again the large man to Susan's left crumpled as the bullet sped through him and towards her left side. But this time the rainbow shards cascaded down her vision just as she felt the beginnings of the impact. . . .

Sirens. Distant. Faint, but coming closer.

Susan clutched her purse as she swivelled on her heels toward the gunman. He looked away, cocking his head as the faint sound of sirens began to grow louder. Susan saw his gun waiver for just an instant, pointed more towards the floor. Grasping her purse firmly, she measured the distance—just as she did as the pitcher for her high school softball team—and flung it, hard, at the clown's gun hand. The pistol clattered to the floor, going off, but hitting no one.

Suddenly, the large man at Susan's side found his courage and charged the robber, knocking him to the ground and pinning him down, just as the sound of sirens and screeching tires grew to a crescendo outside the building.

The police burst in, guns ready, but quickly lowered them as they saw the would-be robber squirming helplessly under the weight of his very angry captor. As the officers quickly cuffed the assailant and gathered up his weapon, Susan and the hefty gentleman found themselves surrounded by the other customers, thanking them, praising them for their courage and quick-wittedness.

Susan wasn't sure she was all that quick-witted, and she had felt more desperate than courageous when she hurled her purse at the man's gun hand. She hadn't wanted to be shot—again. Pleasant as it might have been to be considered a hero, she felt a strange chill shake her body, and she had to sit down in a lobby chair to keep her legs from trembling. She certainly didn't feel heroic. She felt numb, exhausted. She didn't know which scared her more—her close calls or the strange time-jumping effect she seemed to be experiencing.

After giving her account to one of the officers—minus the mysterious time episodes—Susan slowly made her way back to her small Volkswagon and sat for several minutes before starting the car, desperately hoping that no new catastrophes awaited her. She just wanted to go home to the relative safety of her room and the comforting presence of her parents and her younger brother.

She heaved a deep sigh of relief when she pulled into the driveway and got out of the car. *So far, so good.*

She made it to her room without further incident and collapsed onto her bed. Taking several shaky breaths that soon turned to tears, she buried her face in her pillow and sobbed out her fear and emotional mayhem until sleep overtook her.

* * * *

"Honey, wake up! Are you all right?"

Susan opened her eyes. Her overhead light was on, and her mom and dad were standing beside her bed. Her brother Joseph peered around the doorframe at her.

"I . . ." She swallowed and sat up. "I think so. It's been a rather stressful day."

"I should think it was! You were present at a bank robbery! You could have been killed!" Her mother sat down on the side of her bed and smoothed back the auburn hair from her forehead, just like she used to do when Susan was a little girl.

"Um . . . I suppose so." How could she tell her parents that she had been shot—twice? That if not for the bizarre time-altering events that kept happening to her, she might indeed be dead.

"You were very brave—disarming that man as you did." Her father gazed at her with proud eyes.

She didn't feel brave. She felt afraid . . . very afraid. She wanted desperately to tell them all what happened, but how could she do that without sounding . . . insane?

"You're on the local news," Joseph added, stepping into the room, leaning against the doorframe. "I'm brother to a famous sister."

Infamous, is more like it—if people knew what really happened, Susan thought, but outwardly, she gave a wan smile and shrugged.

"Well, if you're up to it, dinner's ready." Her mother stood up and moved to the side.

Susan didn't really feel hungry, but she knew her family would worry if she didn't come down to join them. "Oh, and a gentleman called to ask if he could speak with you tomorrow. Said he was from—let's see—the Starmoor Institute. I didn't recognize it as one of the schools to which you applied, but then you might be getting all sorts of offers from various colleges and universities as your story spreads."

Susan let out a breath. That's all she needed right now. Fame. Just when she wanted to crawl under her covers and not come out.

Her mother's brow furrowed in concern.

"I told him it was all right to drop by. Was that okay? Are you sure you're all right? You look tired. Oh!" Her mother stopped. "What with all the excitement, I forgot to ask about your interview at Pritchard's. Did it go okay?"

Susan swung her feet over the edge of the bed and stood up. "It's iffy. I need references from Tiffani at church and Wantamelee's Camp Director by tomorrow. Right now, I don't care whether I get the position or not."

She sighed. "You're right. I *am* tired, but maybe things will perk up after a good supper."

Her mother put her arm around her. "Well, I've no doubt you'll land a good summer job after all this. Let's get some food in you."

Susan did indeed feel better after a dinner of fried clams—her favorite—fries, coleslaw, and a cherry parfait. It was obvious her mother had fixed a special dinner just for her. Still, she went to bed early and slept deep and dreamless.

* * * *

"Miss Roberts, my name is Jonathan Daniels from the Starmoor Institute. It's a great pleasure to meet you."

Susan studied the man sitting on the couch across from her. In his thirties with dark brown hair and matching eyes and a thin moustache, he was rather handsome to look at.

"Not everyone possesses the talents you have," he continued.

Susan smiled. "Throwing purses at armed robbers is not a talent. It's called desperation."

"That's not what I meant."

"Oh?" Susan suddenly found the man's beautiful brown eyes were a little more intense than felt comfortable.

"Miss Roberts, the Starmoor Institute is both an Academy and a College that caters to students with— shall we say—*unique* talents and abilities. Under certain circumstances, we can trace anomalies given off in the presence of these abilities.

"Yesterday, our system logged several temporal disturbances here in the town of West Chesterton. It didn't take much guesswork to figure out who triggered our alarms once we tapped into the local news."

Susan felt herself grow cold. She glanced back at the kitchen where her mother was busy fixing . . . something. *Keeping out of the way*, as she would put it. Slowly, Susan brought her eyes back to Jonathan Daniels.

"Who are you?" she whispered, clenching her hands.

"Let's just say, I was once a student of the Academy, and now I teach at the College. I am a person of special talent myself."

Again, she glanced back at the kitchen. She felt like screaming irrationally, but bit her tongue. Her hands began to tremble.

"Would you like to know what I can do?"

She wasn't sure she did. But she gasped as a brilliant ball of crackling energy suddenly appeared in his right hand, which he tossed from hand to hand. The smell of ionized oxygen permeated the room. Suddenly, he clenched his fist, and it disappeared.

He smiled.

"I can use this as a weapon or a shield or—with a much smaller voltage—start a dead battery for your car. Now," he leaned forward, lowering his voice. "How many jumps did you have to make before subduing the gunman?"

"Jumps?" She was shivering all over now, heart thumping with a mixture of fear and—and what? Anticipation? Excitement? Insanity?

"We call them *jumps* . . . a leap backwards through time."

Susan's breath came in heavy gasps. He *knew*, he knew what was happening to her. She swallowed, trying to rein in her excitement—or terror. She wasn't sure which.

"Two," she whispered. "But it also happened at my job interview and when I was hit by a pickup. It's like things restarted, and I could avoid the incident or change it."

Jonathan Daniels nodded. His smiled widened. "You're a time-jumper, Miss Roberts! We can teach you how to control it, use it, and above all, protect yourself and others with it."

His smile faded and his face grew serious. "We specialize in producing people who care, Miss Roberts, who will put the good of others above themselves. Like you did with that little girl."

Susan didn't know what to say.

The man continued. "I understand you hope to take over your aunt's business when she retires. That might be possible, but I warn you, if you decide to attend the Starmoor Institute, you might find your goals change, your vision alters—that there is more to living than simply getting ahead."

He sat back, his smile returning. "Are you interested?"

Heart hammering, Susan took a deep breath and nodded.

"I think my vision is already changing," she said quietly. "That happens when you almost die three times and watch it happen to others. When do your classes start?"

Jonathan Daniels' smile stretched wider. "Whenever you're ready. We keep a rather flexible schedule."

"How much will it cost?" Susan mentally ran through her combined savings and checking accounts, and it didn't add up to more than a semester's worth at the local college.

"Just your willingness to come."

She blinked.

He shrugged and grinned. "It's well funded by those who want to see good in this world."

He leaned forward, rolling a tiny energy ball through his fingers. "Shall I have them prepare a dorm room for you?"

Susan paused. This would change everything. She cocked her head and watched the brilliant light play over his fingers. "Yes. The sooner the better."

The man flicked the energy droplet into nothing and stood. He held out his hand. "Miss Sarah Cushings—the Women's Dean—and I will pick you up next Tuesday. And welcome to the fold, Miss Roberts."

Susan took his hand tentatively, fearing a jolt or shock. All she felt was his warmth. She smiled. "I'll be ready."

Angels of Mercy: Strength in Numbers

BY

Jonathan M. Rudder

Two Years Ago....
"Freak!"
"Man, get a load of that guy!"
"Yeah . . . what's up, Quasimodo?"

Fifteen-year-old Trent Prescott gave the group of seven or eight bullies the most cursory of glances as he hobbled along, his shoulders and back a massive bulge beneath the black, leather duster he wore constantly to cover what many perceived as a terrible deformity. The group consisted mainly of boys, with maybe a girl or two—one of them was hard to distinguish—varying in age from around fourteen to eighteen. A fairly broad range of ethnicities were represented, as well.

Trent raised a brow. *The Hunchback of Notre Dame* was on the summer reading list. Apparently one of them was actually doing his homework.

Trent shook his head. He had heard it all before. Sometimes the cat-calls were followed up by foodstuffs, small stones, or other less pleasant projectiles. He pretended to be embarrassed and despondent, but he knew the mockery inspired by his perceived deformity was nothing compared to the fear the truth behind his bulging back would have precipitated. There were times when he had been tempted to rip off his jacket and reveal the truth, but despite the occasional, completely normal bout of anger, he was a gentle soul and wished no harm upon anyone.

And so, he kept his secrets to himself and allowed everyone else to think whatever they would.

Happily, this time, the mockery was not accompanied by a physical display of false superiority, and he hobbled along down the park path. However, before he had gone much further, the cat-calls directed at him stopped abruptly as the bullies' attention was drawn to the next unfortunate to meander down the path.

"*Hey!*" one of the younger boys called out. "*There's Barney Bedwetter!*"

Trent spun around with surprising agility. He saw the bullies descending on a thin, pale-faced boy, with dark, slicked-back hair that glistened with a wet sheen, like he had just climbed out of a pool. The boy frowned, head bowed so that he looked at them through his furrowed brow. Trent guessed that he was maybe ten or eleven.

The bullies encircled their victim.

"Let me go," Trent heard the boy mumble.

"*Let me go!*" one of the bullies mocked. The teenager gave the boy a hard shove and the group started laughing.

"Look at him sweat!" Another sneered, pointing at the boy's face.

An older youth, who appeared to be the ringleader of the group, crossed his arms. "Wonder how long it'll take before he pees his pants. . . ."

That comment seemed to anger their young victim, rather than instill fear.

"Leave me alone!" the boy snarled. It seemed to Trent that the boy was starting to sweat more profusely, though it was hard to tell at that distance.

"Not until you pee yourself, Barney B," the ringleader replied. "Maybe you need some motivation."

One of the older bullies grabbed the boy from behind, pinning his arms to his sides and lifting him from the ground. The boy thrashed, but was not strong enough to break free. The ringleader stepped forward, blocking Trent's view.

Trent was tempted to intervene, concerned that the bullies were going to cross a line that would only end badly for everyone, but stopped when one of them gleefully shouted, "*There he goes!*"

The comment was followed by uproarious laughter, which was cut short when the ringleader took a startled step back. "Dude . . . what the . . . ?"

Trent's gaze fell upon the boy, who had stopped struggling. What had at first appeared to be heavy perspiration was now oozing out of the boy's every pore, drenching his clothing. The boy slipped easily from his captor's grasp, landing on his feet.

"Stop him!" the ringleader shouted.

The bullies scrambled to recapture the boy, but none of them could get a firm grip on him. He slipped through their fingers and arms with ease, finally sliding past the ringleader, charging down the path past Trent, who raised a hand to protect his face from the stray droplets which followed in the boy's wake.

Trent rubbed the liquid between the tips of his fingers. It was extremely slick and had an iridescent sheen. He sniffed at his fingers. The liquid had a faint odor that he could not identify.

He raised his eyes as the bullies charged up to him.

"Hey, Quasimodo, why didn't you stop him?" the ringleader snapped. "He's a *freak!*"

The way the older youth said *freak*, while no less derogatory, was significantly different than when the bullies had used it in reference to him. The utter revulsion in both his voice and expression were unmistakable.

Trent cocked his head, keeping his eyes fixed firmly on the ringleader. "By *freak*, I presume you mean *Genate*."

"Yeah, whatever," the youth shot back. "He's dangerous, and you let him go!"

Brows raised, Trent thrust a thumb in the direction the boy had fled. "*He's* dangerous? Seems to me, you were the ones doing the bullying."

The ringleader, who stood a good five inches taller than Trent, stepped closer to glare down at him. "You some kind of freak-lover?"

A thin smile creased Trent's lips. "At least I don't have a urine fetish."

The bully's face darkened like a storm cloud ready to burst.

Trent was prepared to defend himself, even though it would mean breaking the cover that he and his father had worked so hard and long to create. Fortunately, he did not have to.

"Mr. Trent, is there a problem?"

Two imposing men in suits and sunglasses, with Bluetooth receivers in their ears, strode up to flank him.

Trent cast a sidelong glance at the man on his right, then fixed his gaze once more on the teenager in front of him. "No, Rico. Just a little misunderstanding. We're cool. Aren't we. . . ?"

The ringleader's gaze nervously flicked back and forth between Trent's bodyguards, but he hesitated to reply. Clearly, he did not want to lose face in front of his self-styled gang, so he refused to stand down, but the situation had clearly been reversed.

The one girl Trent was certain about suddenly exclaimed, "Oh my gosh! I've seen him on TV! He's Trent Prescott . . . his dad is, like, David Prescott, the billionaire."

The ringleader blanched and took a step back, raising his hands in front of him. "Yeah, yeah, we're cool. Just a misunderstanding."

Still wearing a tight smile, Trent inclined his head to the bully.

Rico straightened up. "Good to know, Mr. Trent. I guess there's nothing to see here?"

"Yeah," the ringleader stammered. "Nothing to see."

He flicked his head, and he and his gang backed off, retreating from the area.

"You okay, Mr. Trent?" Rico asked again.

Trent gave him a quick nod. "Yeah. I wasn't in any danger. I could have flattened those goons."

"I know, Mr. Trent," the bodyguard replied stiffly. "But it's my job to see that you don't have to. Imagine what would happen if you did. . . ."

Trent smirked. "You don't have to remind me, Rico. Don't worry . . . I won't be careless."

He looked down at the path, his gaze tracking the oily, iridescent trail left in the wake of the boy's escape. He turned to follow the path, but found himself restrained by Rico's meaty hand.

"Going somewhere, Mr. Trent?" the bodyguard asked. "Haven't you had enough adventures for one day?"

Trent glanced at the hand on his shoulder, which Rico abruptly removed. He looked up at the man in grim determination. "I have to find that boy, Rico. I need to make sure he gets home safely. I mean, it's not like he can hide the fact that he's a Genate right now."

Rico frowned. "Mr. Trent. . . ."

Trent sighed. "I'll keep my transponder on . . . pick me up when I signal. Just keep out of sight."

Rico hesitated, then gave Trent a quick nod. He and his partner retreated to the limo parked at the parkside curb.

Trent followed the oily trail out of the park, and though it did eventually start to thin out, it never fully vanished. That came as no surprise. The boy—Trent hesitated to think of him as *Barney*, being fairly certain that was not his real name—had exuded so much of the substance that it would take a while to dissipate or dry up.

The trail led into a rough-looking neighborhood, comprised mainly of multi-family units. It became increasingly obvious that, despite his young age, the boy was clever, accustomed to finding escape routes with the least visibility. The trail eventually led into an alleyway, which Trent was sure led to a dead-end. At first, he assumed the boy's home could be accessed from the alley, but as he continued along it, he noticed something disturbing. At a few points, the oily trail was broken and smeared, as though someone had stepped in the substance and slipped.

Someone else was following the boy.

Trent slowly hobbled along, coming at last within view of the expected dead-end . . . only he could see that the path ahead did in fact T out to either side. He hoped that perhaps his original instinct was wrong and that there was another exit from the alley, but the voice he heard to the left as he neared the T told him otherwise.

"*Please . . . leave me alone!*" he heard the boy plead.

The voice that responded was not what Trent expected. It was gentle, very youthful, and distinctly feminine. "Don't be afraid. We're not here to hurt you, Cory . . . we're here to help."

A third voice joined in, this one with the rasp and crackle of a voice in the process of changing. "Yeah . . . we're freaks, too."

Trent ventured to peek around the corner. He saw the boy—*Cory*, he reminded himself—backed up to a wall, with nowhere to go. In front of him, about ten feet away, stood a pair of kids, whom he judged to be a couple years younger than himself. Perhaps twelve or thirteen, he guessed.

The girl's fine, blonde hair was straight, but unevenly cut and about shoulder length. Her dingy, powder-blue tank-top and dirt-smudged, khaki shorts sagged on her slender, nearly malnourished frame.

The boy—or so Trent presumed—was a little shorter than the girl, but his torn, red muscle-shirt and hole-ridden shorts exposed broad shoulders and a chiseled musculature that many varsity athletes would have envied. His fine, blonde curls, however, almost completely contrasted his athletic physique. If Trent had seen him in a photograph, he would have assumed the picture had been Photoshopped. He had no doubt the boy was a Genate.

Trent caught a glimpse of the girl's vixenish face and stunning blue eyes as she glared at her companion. Turning her attention back to Cory, she said, "Ignore Billy. He's a moron. We're not freaks, and neither are you. Our boss, Arturis, says we're special . . . we're better than the Powerless."

Trent's brow lowered in concern. *Arturis. . . .*

It was a name he had heard before in conversations between his father, the FBI, and his father's own investigators . . . and never used in a pleasant way. He knew it was time to intervene. Something told him that this encounter had a greater chance of ending badly for Cory than his brush with the bullies.

Cory hesitated, processing the girl's words. "I . . . I don't know."

"Come on," the boy named Billy urged. "We'll show you. Arturis . . . he cares about kids like us. He knows things . . . like how your parents locked you up in the basement when they found out you had powers. He wants to help you learn to control your powers, so you don't have to be afraid anymore."

Trent's jaw clenched. That was an argument he had heard used by too many villains, powered or not, to convince Genates to go with them willingly, often never to be seen again.

Fortunately, the line had not been lost on Cory, either. Trent saw a flicker of fear cross his face. He shook his head. "No . . . no, I don't want to. . . ."

Billy's greyish blue eyes flicked towards the girl, and he quirked his lip. "Guess he's not going to listen to reason."

"Be careful, Billy," the girl warned. "He's one of us . . . he's not an enemy."

Trent knew he could not wait another moment and stepped around the corner. In a firm voice, he announced, "The kid said no. Leave him be."

Cory's young accosters spun to face him. They clearly were taken aback by his hunchbacked appearance, which even drew a brief glimmer of pity from their expressions. But the pity was fleeting.

Billy thrust his fists into the side of the dumpster next him. Trent immediately regretted confronting them openly, as the boy effortlessly raised the steel container over his head. "This ain't none of your business. You got ten seconds to get your freaky butt out of here."

The girl bit her lip, as she thoughtfully examined Trent. She reached a hand out towards her friend. "Billy, wait. I don't think anyone needs to get hurt."

Billy gave her an uncertain frown, but lowered the dumpster back to the ground.

The girl cocked her head, her eyes fixed on Trent, and smiled sweetly. "You're one of us, too . . . aren't you?"

The way she said it was more of a statement than a question.

"I'm betting you have a harder time fitting in than most of us," she continued. "You could come, too. Arturis would make sure no one would ever make fun of you again."

Trent grimaced. *Sweet kid, but totally misguided.*

He shook his head. "I think you actually believe what you're saying, but I've heard of this Arturis guy. My father suspects he's behind the disappearances of homeless Genates . . . his investigators say they've found evidence that he's been experimenting on them."

"Investigators?" Billy sputtered, reaching for the dumpster again. "You spying for the Powerless?"

"No," Trent said calmly. "My father funds *legal* endeavors to protect Genates."

The girl blinked at him, as though suddenly recognizing him. "Wait . . . I know you. . . ."

Trent curled his lip. "Let me guess . . . you saw me with my father on TV."

She shook her head. "No."

The girl glanced at Billy. "He's that Prescott guy's son . . . the rich dude that runs the shelter. . . ."

Billy, though still wary, fully removed his hands from the dumpster. "Your dad seems like a good guy . . . for a Powerless. What're you doing here? You out on a mercy mission for the shelter?"

Trent inclined his head towards Cory. "Nope. I saw him get ambushed by some bullies in the park and followed him. Wanted to make sure he was okay."

"He's fine," the girl said. "Trust me . . . Arturis isn't what your dad thinks. . . ."

"Yeah," Billy interrupted. "He takes real good care of us freaks. He's the only who really cares. . . ."

Trent raised his brow again. "Really? You've met Arturis?"

Billy blustered again, his dirty face turning red. "Well, no, but. . . ."

"Ah," Trent responded. "I see. He shows his concern by having his cronies make sure you have a place to sleep and plenty of food to eat."

Billy's mouth continued to work fruitlessly. "Well, no . . . but they pay us. . . ."

"To kidnap innocent kids and watch them vanish?" Trent finished for him. "Sounds like a really caring guy."

Though his gaze was fixed on Billy, Trent could see the girl out of the corner of his eye. She was biting her lip so hard that he thought it might start bleeding at any moment.

Finally, she shook her head. "I'm sorry. We have to take Cory to Arturis . . . he has to see that Arturis only wants to help him."

Trent looked directly at Cory. "You want to go with them, Cory?"

The boy, his eyes wide, swallowed and shook his head.

Trent glanced between the two would-be kidnappers. "There you go . . . he doesn't want to go."

The girl looked genuinely remorseful as she replied, "It isn't his choice, nor ours. He's coming with us."

"And you can't stop us," Billy snapped.

As they turned to take Cory into custody, Trent ripped open the front of his shirt, thankful it had snaps instead of buttons. In a matter of seconds, a light began to burn from within his chest, manifesting as a radiant beam—almost like molten gold in appearance—bursting forth. It shot between Billy and the girl, then flowed out between the walls of the buildings flanking the alley, forming a blockade of solid energy between Cory and his assailants.

"You're not taking him anywhere," Trent gritted. He knew he had done it. Whoever Arturis was, he would soon know that Trent was a Genate . . . and he had no doubt that the rest of the world would find out soon after.

Billy and the girl both spun around, shocked looks on their faces. Though Billy seemed half-inclined to grab the dumpster again, he hesitated, which told Trent that he was not quite ready to find out what else he could do.

"All right," the girl said at last, motioning for Trent to stand down. "We'll let Cory go . . . just to show you we're not monsters."

Trent relaxed, and his energy beam dissipated. "I didn't doubt that for a moment . . . but I do doubt this Arturis you keep talking about. But it doesn't matter. Cory's safe."

He smiled and nodded at the wall behind the two younger kids.

Billy and the girl looked, gaping. Cory was gone, the only sign of his former presence a long, iridescent streak of oily slime ascending the wall.

Trent took advantage of the distraction to slip around the corner, completely pulling off his shirt and duster, revealing a strong, toned torso—though not nearly as defined as Billy's—and more. He stretched his white-feathered wings and launched himself into the air, landing atop the building. He tucked his clothes in his backpack and crept to the edge of the roof, peering down into the alley.

After the two young Genates looked around for him, Billy finally turned to the girl and said, "What now? You know Cravitz is gonna take it out on *us*. . . ."

The girl put her hands on her scrawny hips, her head bowed in thought. After a moment, she looked at Billy. Trent could see anxiety in her face, but she remained calm. "We'll just tell him the truth."

She glanced around the alley once more, then said, "We'd better get to the meeting place."

"Then let's get outta here," Billy said, placing his fingers against his temples. His eyes began to glow yellow as his feet slowly lifted from the ground.

Levitation, Trent thought. *Interesting power combination. . . .*

"Wait," the girl said abruptly. She hesitated a moment, an uncertain, almost guilty look on her face. "Billy, don't say anything about Prescott. We'll just say it was another freak."

"What?" Billy exclaimed. "Why?"

The girl blushed, bringing a look of astonishment to Billy's face, which melted into a mischievous grin. "Oh my gosh, Jackie! You have a crush on the hunchbacked dork!"

Trent stifled a chuckle. He was flattered, but he could not take her seriously . . . she was just a kid. *Cute.*

Apparently, the girl—Jackie—did not agree. With an indignant scowl, she reached a hand out to grab at Billy, who easily dodged and rose above her head. "I'll turn you into fertilizer, Billy Drake!"

"Only if you can catch me!" Billy laughed. He rose faster, suddenly shooting into the air in a streak of light, accompanied by the thunder and rattle of a very small sonic boom.

Trent watched him disappear and shook his head, stunned. He was glad that his confrontation had not turned to violence. There was an astonishing amount of power in that small package. He looked back down into the alley at the girl.

Jackie lifted her hands from her sides. They began to glow with a yellow light, and a golden aura surrounded her. To Trent, it seemed as though the air around her was shimmering, rather than an energy projected from her body. The girl launched herself into the air and flew in the direction Billy had gone.

Trent was surprised she had not noticed him on the roof. *Perhaps she was too distracted.*

He stretched his wings and flew off after her, hoping she would lead him to Arturis.

Trent found it challenging to keep her in sight. The girl was fast, though not nearly as fast as her friend. He had to push himself to his limits and soon found himself lagging. Fortunately, she had not gone too far before she dropped into the buildings below.

Trent dove to the rooftops, alighting on a building overlooking the small back parking lot to which Jackie had descended. He crept to the edge of the roof and peeked down to the lot. A dark blue sedan was parked catty-corner across the entrance to the lot, as though to block the kids' escape.

Trent snorted. *They can fly.*

Three men dressed in suits stood outside the vehicle, facing the kids.

The one in front—a short, beefy man with receding brown hair—held his hands out as he spoke in a deeply disappointed voice. "Jackie, Jackie . . . Billy here tells me you let the Vargas boy get away."

Jackie glanced nervously at Billy. "Well, not exactly, Mr. Cravitz. We didn't *let* him get away. Another freak showed up. He had some real power. . . ."

Cravitz gave her a smirk. "Jackie, you and Billy have real power. I don't know many grown-up freaks that have the kind of power you two have."

He shrugged. "But hey, I'm willing to let bygones be bygones."

Jackie and Billy visibly relaxed.

"But," Cravitz continued. "Arturis . . . well, he ain't so amenable. I mean, he's put a lot into you. You've saved so many kids from the streets, and he's grateful . . . but, you know, he's paid a lot for you to do that."

The kids looked nervous, and Trent decided it was time to call for backup. He reached down to his waist and pressed a button on his belt, signaling Rico and Dravecki to pick him up. He tapped the button three more times . . . three short, three long, three short: SOS.

"Hey, we didn't get the kid," Billy said with a nervous smile. "He can, like, keep the money."

Trent's brow lowered in confusion. Besides flight, he had no idea what Jackie could do, but he was fairly certain Billy could have made short work of Cravitz and his goons.

Cravitz's brown brows shot up. "Oh, there's no doubt about that, Billy-boy. But, you know, you're gonna have to do a lot better. That's three that's got away in the last week alone. You're getting soft."

Jackie frowned. She seemed to lose a little of her fear. "Look, Mr. Cravitz, they were afraid. Sometimes, they don't get it. They don't believe *anyone* wants to help. . . ."

Cravitz gave her a serpentine smile. "That's why you gotta *make* 'em see sometimes."

Jackie glanced at Billy, then said, "The freak who helped Cory today . . . he said Arturis is kidnapping these kids to experiment on them."

Billy puffed up his chest, putting on a false air of confidence. "Yeah, Cravitz. You said he only wants to help . . . what about it? We're not in this to hurt anyone."

"Oho!" Cravitz exclaimed in mock disbelief. He chuckled and wiped his hand across his face. "Look, kid, I know you're not the brightest bulb, but are you serious? You don't ask questions . . . and you sure as heck don't cross Arturis."

He thrust his hands in his pockets. "Geordi, Mack . . . I think it's time they meet the boss."

Trent reached into a side pouch on his backpack and pulled out a white ski-mask he kept on hand for emergencies, then slipped it on. *Come on, Rico. . . .*

Cravitz's goons both reached into their jackets and pulled out pistols that looked like they belonged in a sci-fi movie. Trent dove off the roof of the building and swooped down, pouring all of his energy behind his force blast. He focused on forming a shield wall between Cravitz and the kids. Every muscle in his body strained against the effort. He had never tried to form a wall that size before, and it took every ounce of his strength.

Cravitz jumped back in alarm as the golden wall formed before him. "What the. . . ? Who is this punk?"

"Get out of here!" Trent called to the kids in a strained voice. "I'll hold them off."

Cravitz pointed up at Trent, who awkwardly hovered well above his force wall like a hummingbird with the wings of an albatross. "Take him down!"

Cravitz's goons took aim at Trent.

Billy and Jackie exchanged a conflicted glance that reflected both the urge to flee and the desire to help their rescuer. With a quick nod from Jackie, Billy put his fingers to his temples and squeezed his eyes shut just as Cravitz's men opened fire.

Trent was not sure what to expect, but whatever projectiles or energy the high-tech weapons fired was both silent and invisible. His shield wall instantly dissipated as his chest beam was blocked by an unseen force. Unfortunately for him, the unexpected interruption did not allow him time to refocus his efforts, and his own energy backlashed on him. The golden force hammered into him, knocking him senseless.

The last thing he remembered before blacking out was freefalling through the air. . . .

* * * *

Trent slowly blinked his eyes open, his head throbbing. He was lying in bed, his covers tucked up under his arms, his wings gently cradling his body. As he came to full consciousness, he realized that his entire body was throbbing. His memories of the previous day were foggy at best, and he could remember nothing about the evening, including how he ended up in bed, nor why he hurt so badly.

He groaned, allowing his head to roll to the side. Trent blinked at the two faces staring back at him mere inches from his own. A boy and a girl, perhaps two or three years younger than himself, leaned with their chins on their arms on the edge of his bed. Both pink-cheeked faces were framed by clean, blonde hair. The girl's was straight, bobbed just above her shoulders. The boy's was curly, though very light and fine.

Their blue eyes were fraught with concern.

Trent's eyes flicked from one face to the other. *Who. . . ?*

Memories started flooding back—his encounter with the bullies in the park, the Genate runaway, the super-powered street rats, the Mafia wannabes . . . all of it. Trent blinked again. The faces before him were the street rats, Billy and Jackie, though he hardly recognized them.

Groaning, he dragged himself up into a sitting position. He glanced at the younger kids again, who both stood to their feet. Jackie was attired in a clean, blue blouse and slacks. Billy wore a pale green button-up shirt and khakis. Trent reached out and plucked at the collar of Jackie's blouse.

"I see Alice got her hands on you two," he rasped, letting his hand drop. "What happened? Why didn't you get out of there?"

Jackie's cheeks reddened. "We couldn't . . . I mean, you were right. Cravitz and his crew pretty much admitted that everything you said was true."

"And even after I tried to trash you, you came to our rescue," Billy added. "We couldn't let Cravitz take you down."

Blushing, he gave Trent a nervous shrug. "Guess I took you down anyway."

Trent's brows shot up. "That was you? I thought those goons shot me."

"They tried," Jackie explained. "But Billy surrounded you with a force field."

Billy frowned at her. "It's not a *force field* . . . it's a telekinetic bubble."

The girl grimaced back. "Whatever, dork. Anyway, their neutralizers couldn't pierce it. Unfortunately, neither could your energy beam . . . it kinda backfired. Knocked you out cold."

"How'd you stop them?" Trent asked.

"We didn't," Billy replied. "Your bodyguards came flying around the corner in that crazy limo of yours and hopped out, guns blazing. Neutralizers don't have an effect on Powerless, and they didn't have a chance to pull their real guns."

Jackie nodded energetically. "Cravitz and his men had to take cover, so Billy was able to grab you, and we booked it to the limo. Your guy, Rico . . . he brought us here."

She paused, her expression sobering. "He said your dad gives money to a bunch of homes and schools, other than the shelter, that help kids like us . . . you know, freaks."

"Genates," Trent replied emphatically. He hated the term *freak*. He leaned his head back and closed his eyes. "Yeah. He has reason to care."

Jackie and Billy both frowned, and Jackie quietly said, "You're actually kind of lucky . . . you have a dad who cares. A lot of us are like Cory. His parents treat him like some kind of monster. . . ."

"And then there are those like us," Billy added. "We'd be happy enough just to have parents, whether or not they treat us like monsters."

"I've already told you two," a man's gentle voice interjected. "You have a home, if you want it."

Trent turned his gaze towards his bedroom door. His father, David Prescott, stood there, leaning on the frame with one hand. He wore a brown cashmere sweater over a blue button-up shirt and a pair of khakis. His short hair, combed to the side, was almost completely white, despite topping a face that belonged to a man in his early to mid-forties. With his free hand, he adjusted his black-rimmed glasses.

"From what Rico tells me, you saved my son's life, when you could have just as easily escaped," Mr. Prescott continued. "That speaks volumes to me about your honor and integrity."

Trent nodded in agreement. "It's true, Dad. Before everything went south, I saw them stand up to Arturis' henchmen. I think if it had been Arturis himself, they would have told him where to get off."

Nodding thoughtfully, Mr. Prescott looked at the floor, rubbing his chin. He glanced sideways at his son. "Trent, you feel up to showing your friends the gym?"

For a moment, Trent forgot his aches and pain. "You bet!"

Mr. Prescott gave him a quick nod. "Good. Get dressed and meet me downstairs."

After Trent's father departed, Billy quipped, flexing his bicep, which strained against the loose sleeve of his dress shirt, "Do I look like I need a gym?"

Trent grinned at him. "Just wait."

He threw back his covers, momentarily forgetting the presence of a girl in his bedroom—then thankful that whoever had put him in his bed had been cognizant enough to attire him in pajama bottoms—and gingerly slid himself into position to stand. As he attempted to rise to his feet, his muscles loudly reminded him of the trauma inflicted on his body the day before, and his knees startled to buckle.

Billy caught him and lifted him to his feet, offering his slight, but seriously muscular frame as support. While Trent had witnessed the boy's immense strength in action firsthand, he was still astounded by the sense of physical fortitude he felt when leaning against Billy.

It was almost like leaning on a statue chiseled from solid granite. The boy did not have to exert himself at all to keep Trent aright.

"Thanks," Trent said to Billy, wearing a sheepish grin. "I may have been a little hasty."

Billy snorted rudely. "Eh, whatever."

Trent could see a hint of delight flash across the boy's face, despite the tough façade he weakly maintained. *No one's probably ever thanked him for anything.*

He allowed Billy to help him to his dresser and closet, where he collected some fresh clothing. All the while, he could feel Jackie's gaze on him. He couldn't help but crack a smile to himself. No one had ever admired him for his physique before. Of course, no one other than his parents or the household staff had ever actually seen him as he truly was. To the outside world, he was the hobbled, severely hunchbacked son of David Prescott.

"What's so funny?" Billy asked.

Trent shuffled through his closet and pulled out a grey dress shirt. "It's nothing."

Billy shot a look over his shoulder at Jackie and broke into a grin. "Ohhh! Almost forgot Jackie's sweet on you."

"Billy Drake!" Jackie shouted, face livid.

Trent spun around just as the girl grabbed the wind-up alarm clock on his night table—a low-tech accessory, but one he prized—with her left hand. The clock vanished in a blaze of golden light, which she absorbed into her body and released through her outstretched hand. The golden beam struck Billy in the back and flung him forward into the closet. A mountain of clothes, dragged off their hangers by the boy's passage, avalanched upon him. From somewhere within the pile, Trent could hear the muffled ring of his clock's alarm.

Trent stared in shock at the pile of clothing, frozen for a moment by the girl's violent outburst. He fell to his knees to dig Billy out from under the clothes.

"Oh, don't worry about him," Jackie grumped. "He can take way more than I can dish out."

The pile of clothing started to jiggle as Billy broke into laughter. The boy clambered out from beneath the mound, grinning broadly. As he stepped out of the closet, Trent could see that the blast had not left a mark on Billy's shirt.

Mainly concussive, like my energy. Trent turned his gaze on Jackie. "Matter transmutation?"

Jackie blushed and shrugged. "I . . . I guess. If that means I can turn things into energy, then yeah. But the effects don't last very long."

Trent picked up his clock and shut off the alarm. A quick examination revealed that it had fully reverted to its original state, including the scratches and dings incurred over time.

"Huh," he uttered in an interested fashion, then tossed the clock back to Jackie, who deftly caught it.

Picking up the clothes he had picked out, he limped into his bathroom to change. He could flatten his wings fairly well against his body, but his clothing still had to be designed to hide them the best way possible, and a shirt alone could not disguise the entirety of his wings, so he always wore his duster when he went out. His hobbled gate was only partially an act. It was also partially an effort to keep his duster from swinging too wide and revealing the lower portions of his wings that could not be constrained by clothing . . . at least, not without a significant amount of discomfort.

Once he was dressed, Trent hobbled out of the bathroom towards his bedroom door, motioning for Jackie and Billy to follow him. His room was located at the end of a hallway, which terminated in a wall fully occupied by an oversized portrait of a kindly old woman in Victorian dress. Across the hall from his room was a guest room, where he assumed the kids had been put up for the night.

He paused in front of the portrait and waited for Jackie and Billy to join him.

Billy pointed at the portrait. "Like, what's up with the old woman? Kind of creepy, if you ask me."

"No one asked you," Jackie shot back. "I think she looks kind of . . . I don't know. Warm?"

Trent half-smiled. "That's my great-great . . . well, several greats aunt, Priscilla Prescott. She advocated for children in England, fighting against the workhouses. She's got a lot of secrets. Let's check out the gym. . . ."

He reached to one edge of the portrait and pressed his fingers against a sensor on the back of the frame. With a *click*, the portrait swung outward, revealing a metal door, which split down the middle and slid back, revealing an elevator.

Billy looked quizzical. "You keep the elevator to the gym behind a picture?"

Trent nodded them into the elevator. "You'll see."

The three teenagers piled into the elevator, which made a rather slow descent into a sub-basement located well beneath the surface floors of Prescott Manor. When the kids stepped out of the elevator, Billy and Jackie gasped in awe. They found themselves standing just inside a massive, high-ceilinged chamber, tiled completely from floor to ceiling with metal plates with a surface area of about an inch.

"What the heck kind of gym is this?" Billy exclaimed. Surprisingly, his voice did not echo. He shouted loudly, "Hey!" but still there was no echo.

"The tiles have a sound dampening property," Trent explained. "Without it, the echo in here would be almost deafening."

High up in the far wall, a large portion of the tiles began to shift and fold back against themselves with the sound of falling dominos, revealing a long window, through which could be seen some sort of control room. Mr. Prescott sat at a control board in front of the window. He leaned forward and spoke into a microphone. His voice emanated from unseen speakers positioned throughout the chamber. "Would you like to give them a brief demonstration, Trent?"

Trent grinned. "Be right back, guys."

He trotted across the *gym* and through a sliding door that appeared from behind another set of shifting tiles. The door opened into a locker room, replete with several rows of lockers—only one of which was in active use—shower stalls, and other common locker room amenities. He stripped off his clothes and stuffed them in his locker, then pulled out his workout suit.

It had taken him quite a while to become comfortable with the top, as it had been modeled after a number of women's athletic costumes, especially swimsuits, gymnastics leotards, and figure skating outfits—with a low, open back to accommodate his wings—but he no longer found it discomfiting. It was a necessary evil.

As he donned the suit, he noticed two other suits folded on the bench next him and cracked a slight smile. This was the first time his father had ever invited any of the rescued Genates to stay. Usually, they were funneled to special schools or foster homes, which catered specifically to their needs.

Trent did not mind. He had become very lonely over the years.

He stood up and stretched the kinks out of his wings, then charged for the door, launching himself into the air as he exited the locker room. For a brief moment, he closed his eyes, simply enjoying the exhilaration of flight, but he knew better than to keep them closed . . . the ceiling approached quickly. He swerved just in time to miss a collision and allowed himself to freefall for a couple seconds.

Tiles from the walls and floor shuffled around and formed small turrets, which tracked his movement and opened fire. Bolts of blue energy flashed past him with the lingering odor and taste of ionized oxygen, as he weaved and somersaulted through the air. Walls and other objects of various size and dimensions formed throughout the room, creating a veritable obstacle course.

Trent fired his chest beam, forming a shield wall between two obstacles, which deflected several blasts. When he had adjusted his own angle, he redirected the energy into a concussive beam, which shattered one of the turrets. The component tiles scattered across the floor, causing a ripple to run through the entire room, as they were absorbed back into the chamber's matrix.

He realized very quickly that he had misjudged his angle and flew directly into the line of fire of another turret. He tried to twist in the air, but the blue bolt blasted him squarely between the shoulders, sending a stunning jolt through his body. Completely numbed, he fell through the air, only to be caught by a tangled web of tiles, which formed a safety net beneath him, lowering him gently to the gym floor.

As feeling returned to his body, he groaned and rolled to his feet. He was thankful that the effects of the shock turrets were far less intense than the backlash of his own force beam. He was met at the center of the room by Billy and Jackie, who were beaming with enthusiasm.

"That was *awesome!*" Billy shouted. "Like a real life video game . . . when do we get to try?"

Trent chuckled. "I saw a couple gym suits in the locker room . . . just your size."

Jackie and Billy exchanged excited looks, then charged for the locker room door.

* * * *

Trent, his father, and their young guests sat at the table in the Prescott dining room. *Dining room* was a poor descriptor for the chamber. Dining *hall* would have been a much more apt label. It was almost the size of a small ranch house, decked out in elaborate furnishings and fixtures. The tenor of the room was not fashionably elegant or romantic in anyway, being brightly lit by several modern ceiling fixtures. The Prescotts frequently used the mansion's dining room as a soup kitchen and conference hall.

The Prescotts' household staff went through the motions of their domestic duties, serving dinner to their employers and their young guests, but David Prescott did not stand on formality. As soon as everything was ready, the staff would take their meal at the long dining table, as well. The staff was limited, mainly because Trent and his father agreed that it would be best to minimize knowledge of Trent's genetic abnormalities. The world had reacted extremely to the unusual increase in the Genate population over the last couple of decades. Those born with severe genetic aberrations—resulting sometimes in extreme physical abnormalities, and at other times the development of unusual powers—were greeted by a very large portion of the normal population with the wide-eyed wonder and excitement afforded superpowered heroes.

However, others viewed them with an irrational fear—despite the general acceptance of the Altered, those who obtained powers through incidental or scientific means—often reacting to their presence with derision or open violence, as well as lobbying for their incarceration or extermination. These individuals did not seem to realize how dangerous they themselves had become, and they were a large enough presence to keep most Genates underground.

From there, things only got worse. Scientists abounded, like Arturis, who viewed them with the curiosity afforded a newly-discovered species, chemical element, or disease ... wishing nothing more than to poke, prod, dissect, and often experiment on them. Then there were the multitude of governments, militaries, and radical militias and terrorist organizations, which wanted to recruit them for their own nefarious purposes.

The staff David Prescott had kept on after Trent's mutations began to exhibit were those closest to the family, and thus the most trusted: Alice, the housekeeper, a plain woman in her late fifties, with a distinct Southern drawl; Maxwell, the butler, a portly and proper old gentleman, imported from the Prescotts' holdings in Gloucestershire, England; Belinda, the cook, a recent graduate from one of the most prestigious cooking schools in the Northeastern States; and the Maids, Clarice and Nikita, two young ladies working for the Prescotts while making their way through college—while fairly new to the household, they were Genates themselves and not disposed to reveal Trent's secret. And, of course, there were the security guards, Rico and Dravecki.

Noticeably absent was Trent's mother, Sandra. She had inexplicably died giving birth to him. The autopsy was inconclusive, and the cause of her death remained a mystery, though Trent—regardless of his father's exhortations to the contrary—blamed himself. *He* was the only reasonable catalyst, despite the fact that his powers and mutations did not begin to surface until he was almost eleven.

There were many theories as to the origins of Genates, but no solid evidence to support any of them. One of them, of course, was Evolution—which might have held some water, were the Theory of Evolution itself not so full of holes it could be used as a sprinkler system and almost completely lacking in any conclusive evidence whatsoever. Another was that one or both of the parents had been exposed to some form of radioactive or chemical contaminant that fundamentally changed their DNA. The problem was that, when studied and tested, the parents of Genates frequently showed no sign of genetic mutation.

It *was* true that some Genates were the offspring of at least one parent that was, in fact, an Altered—

someone who had been genetically altered through external means: said exposure to hazardous radiation or chemicals, genetic manipulation, scientific accidents, and so forth. Another known subsection of Genates were the offspring of Extra-terrestrial trysts with humans. Of course, offspring of other Genates often produced Genate children.

However, David Prescott was not an ET, an Altered, nor a Genate, nor was Sandra, as far as anyone could tell. And this held true for the vast majority of Genates, yet the number of Genates emerging had been rising slowly, but steadily for decades. At the outset of the Twenty-first Century, the numbers exploded, though they still made up a small minority of the world's population. There was no unifying genetic or environmental association between any of them.

"So," Trent's father said to Billy and Jackie as dinner began. "This will be the third and last time I make this offer: you are welcome to stay here, if you want. Between the accounts given to me by Trent, Rico, and Dravecki, and from my own conversations with you, I have the sense that you're a couple of good kids that got a raw deal."

He paused, his expression becoming stern. "Just be warned: my house has rules, and they have to be followed, or you can pack your bags."

"Rules?" Billy echoed uncertainly. He and Jackie had been on their own for nearly five years. The idea of rules very obviously did not sit well with him.

Mr. Prescott inclined his head. "Indeed. And, as Trent can tell you, I do not take them lightly. That said, you are free to leave—or I can find you a home to your liking—should you ever feel my rules are unreasonable to you. But if you leave, you won't be coming back. I have enough shelters in the city . . . and those do not include my home."

Jackie poked at her vegetables in conflicted contemplation. At last, she looked up, shooting a glance at Billy, then Trent, before fixing her blue eyes on her host. "Mr. Prescott, sir, I'll confess I'm really uncomfortable with the idea. . . ."

Trent felt a strange pang, which gave him a bit of a start. He hardly knew these orphans, yet he felt a very real connection to them. Perhaps it was just the loneliness of his childhood catching up to him, relieved by the notion of having friends, but he realized he very strongly desired for them to stay.

He could tell by the somewhat surprised and crestfallen look on his father's face that he, too, was somewhat disappointed—undoubtedly because he was acutely aware of Trent's friendlessness.

"But," the girl continued. "I want to stay. . . ."

Billy's eyes grew wide in disbelief.

Jackie's head tilted down a little. "No one's ever been kind to us. No one's ever offered us a home—except a temporary one at your shelter. *Your* shelter. Arturis was just using us . . . but I think *you* really mean it."

She blinked, allowing a quiet tear to escape her eye. "I want a home, Mr. Prescott."

Trent glanced at Billy and saw that he, too, was giving new consideration to his father's offer.

Billy turned a sober eye on David Prescott. "Yes, sir. What she said."

His cheeks reddened a little, his lips cracking into a half-grin, and he shrugged. "Besides, you've got a super-cool house."

With a relieved chuckle, Mr. Prescott leaned forward, folding his hands on the table before him.

Trent raised a brow. He knew that gesture. It usually came before a lecture or a pronouncement of something he did not usually like.

"In all seriousness, though," his father said. "I have a confession of my own to make. What I said before is true—your actions in defense of Trent did demonstrate a high level of honor and integrity in my sight, and my conversations with you revealed a kindness and compassion for others that perhaps you don't even recognize—but my offer was not wholly selfless."

Trent gave his full attention to his father, intrigued.

"First, I make this offer for my son. His youth has been almost entirely void of friendship, and I have already seen the seeds of friendship blooming between you."

Trent felt his cheeks heat up—that was information he wished his father had not bothered to share—but he attempted to maintain his composure.

"Secondly," Mr. Prescott continued. "I want your help."

He glanced at the Butler. "Maxwell, if you would?"

The elderly man slowly rose to his feet and bowed at the shoulders, intoning in his perfect, emotionless, bass voice, "Of course, sir."

As the butler politely stepped away from the table, Mr. Prescott continued. "While you were just trying to survive on the streets, Trent spent the last five years training. With powers like those you three possess, it is inevitable that you will have to make a choice: to use them as pawns for monsters like Arturis, to use them for your own gain—and become Arturis—or to use them for the greater good. I believe that in your hearts, you desire the last, but you have had little to no guidance."

Billy and Jackie's expressions were slowly becoming suspicious. Trent himself was wondering where his father was going with his speech.

"I want to offer you that guidance," Mr. Prescott continued. "I want to teach you how to fully harness your powers, to control them, and to use them for the greater good."

Jackie's sharp-featured face darkened. "You're starting to sound an awful lot like Arturis yourself, Mr. Prescott. . . ."

Mr. Prescott gave her a slight smile. "Yes, I can appreciate how it may sound. My offer is, indeed, similar. From what you have told me, Arturis is stepping up his game. He is recruiting young Genates, like yourselves, to essentially prey on their own kind. I want to stop him. Most of the street kids he captures are never seen again. Those who are have come back . . . *changed*, and not for the better.

"You know that I run the shelter for homeless Genates in the city. I also find homes for kids like yourselves or arrange, at their request only, to send them to special schools, which train them to control their powers and help them merge into society. With Arturis—and others like him—pushing his agenda, many more kids are being lost every day. That has to stop, and I believe you three can make that happen . . . eventually."

Maxwell returned, depositing a plain, white gift-box—the kind stores use when wrapping Christmas presents—in front of each of the three youths.

Jackie and Billy opened theirs right away and looked up, agape.

"It will take hard work," Mr. Prescott continued. "But in time, I think you will be ready to take the fight back to Arturis. . . ."

Trent opened his own box and looked inside, his own eyes widening in wonder.

* * * *

The Present

Cravitz pushed back his white fedora and scratched his balding forehead. A cocky grin split his lips, as he stared at the thirteen-year-old boy plastered against the wall of the alley. Oily slime soaked his body.

"Well, Cory," Cravitz said conversationally. "You've led us on a really long hunt, but it looks like you're not going to . . . er, *slip* past us this time."

His cohorts chuckled at the pun.

Cory looked up and saw two more goons on the roof above him, neutralizers pointed at him. He turned his terrified gaze back on Cravitz, who beckoned to him with one hand.

"Come along quietly, and no one will hurt ya."

Cory took a step forward, hesitated, then fell back against the wall, screaming, "*No!*"

Cravitz sighed, then shrugged. "Ok, have it your own way."

He gave his men a nod, and they opened fire.

A streak of light interjected itself between the thugs and Cory, stopping in front of the boy, materializing as a teenager around fifteen years of age, dressed from head to toe in a white costume. His cowl ended in a mask that covered the upper portion of his face, but left his fine, curly blonde hair visible on top. The top of the cowl was ringed in gold, from which gold stripes ran down the sides of his head to his shoulders, running to his tight, gold gloves. Golden stripes ran up from the tops of his snug, gold boots, meeting at his waist, belt-like, angling downward to a point just below his navel, almost like an M. A golden circle a few inches in diameter decorated the center of his chest. His fingertips were pressed to his temples, eyes blazing with a yellow light.

The invisible pulses from the neutralizers thudded against an equally invisible telekinetic bubble, light shimmering where they hit.

From above the heads of Cravitz and his men, a young, male voice rang out. "You're done, Cravitz. You can tell Arturis that these streets belong to *us* now!"

Cravitz looked up and saw a youth with white wings pumping behind him, dressed in a costume identical to the first youth. Beside him hovered a girl in the same attire, surrounded by a halo of energy.

"You!" Cravitz exclaimed. "Think you're heroes or something? Gonna save Slime-boy from the big, bad gangster?"

"We're not heroes, Cravitz," the girl replied firmly. "We're Angels!"

About the Authors

Jonathan M. Rudder graduated with a BA in English from Southern Illinois University Edwardsville and an MFA in Creative Writing from Full Sail University in Winter Park, FL. He and his brother, Douglas, are co-Publishers and Managing Editors for RudderHaven, based in Granite City, IL. Inspired at an early age by the works of J.R.R. Tolkien and C.S. Lewis, Jonathan became an avid reader—and later writer—of fantasy and science fiction, including *The Milhavior Chronicles*. He served for almost nine years as the copyeditor, writer, and official Tolkien lore-expert for the award-winning MMO *The Lord of the Rings Online* by Time Warner/Turbine Inc, finishing his career there as a content designer. Currently, Jonathan dedicates most of his time to his family, RudderHaven, and teaching in the 5th highest rated game design degree program in the world, located at Becker College, Worcester, MA.

Douglas Rudder is a St. Louis area science fiction and fantasy author. He and his brother, Jonathan, are co-Publishers and Managing Editors for RudderHaven. He currently resides in southern Illinois, where he often battles Orcs, Aliens, and Super-Villains with his wife and daughter. An avid reader of science fiction and fantasy since childhood, Doug's first book, *Tolkien: Roncevaux, Ethandune, and Middle-earth*, is a work of literary criticism. He is also an author and editor for *The RudderHaven Science Fiction and Fantasy Anthology* series. Current creative endeavors include three novels in various stages of mayhem and several short stories for upcoming anthologies.

Becca Lynn Rudder is teenaged girl with a dream of writing a story—and actually finishing one, finally. She is the daughter of Douglas and Sheri Rudder, both of which are also *RudderHaven* authors. They, as well as other members of her family, helped her with the polishing phases of her story. She knows that she couldn't have finished it without their help. Becca lives in southern Illinois with her parents and their dog, Shadow Star. She enjoys MMOs and PC games, movies and TV shows (especially older ones), reading, and just plain talking. She likes Barbies and Princesses—and *really* likes super-heroes, Star Trek/Star Wars, and Lord of the Rings as well.

C.K. Deatherage earned her BA and MA in English Language & Literature from Southern Illinois University Edwardsville and her PhD in Old and Middle English Language & Literature from Purdue University. Her previous publications include *Waysmeet: Poems and Tales* *of Fantasy and Wonder*, 'The Madgician and the Vorpal Sword' in *The RudderHaven Science Fiction and Fantasy Anthology IV,* 'Niall MacDonaugh and the Leipreachan' in *The RudderHaven Science Fiction and Fantasy Anthology I*, 'Final Entry' in *Star Trek: Strange New Worlds V*, and various poems in anthologies and journals. She won the 2013 Poet of the Year and the 2013 Vardis Fisher Award for Most Humorous Piece by the Idaho Writers League. She currently resides in Idaho with her husband, two kids, two large dogs, and four cats—and an occasional, very temporary field mouse.

OTHER ANTHOLOGIES PUBLISHED BY RUDDERHAVEN

The RudderHaven Science Fiction and Fantasy Anthology, Vol I edited by Douglas Rudder
The RudderHaven Science Fiction and Fantasy Anthology, Vol II edited by Douglas Rudder
The RudderHaven Science Fiction and Fantasy Anthology, Vol III edited by Douglas Rudder
The RudderHaven Science Fiction and Fantasy Anthology, Vol IV edited by Douglas Rudder
The RudderHaven Science Fiction and Fantasy Anthology, Vol V edited by Douglas Rudder
Waysmeet: Poems and Tales of Fantasy and Wonder by C.K. Deatherage
Tales with a Twist edited by C.K. Deatherage
Endgame Vol I edited by Jonathan M. Rudder

OTHER FICTION PUBLISHED BY RUDDERHAVEN

Sharamitaro by Jonathan M. Rudder
The Road to Elekar by Jonathan M. Rudder
A Howl on the Wind by Jonathan M. Rudder
The Winds of a Rising Storm by Jonathan M. Rudder
The Flame and the Shadow by Jonathan M. Rudder
The Shadow of the Bear by Larry D. Rudder

RELATED NON-FICTION PUBLISHED BY RUDDERHAVEN

Tolkien: Roncevaux, Ethandune, and Middle-earth by Douglas Rudder

Made in the USA
Lexington, KY
19 September 2017